Irving and Bob

Bob

By Andy Scoville

Contents

Thanks to Paula for forcing me to finish what I started, Lin, Bill and both Chris P and Chris B for the feedback, Kev for the impossible Pear and Bob for the inspiration.

The Watchers

Are you lucky to be alive?

Are you the type of person who leaves the house to go to work but as you step out of the door you realise your shoe is undone?

It may only take half a minute to tie your shoe.

But that thirty seconds means you arrive at the train station or bus stop just as your bus, or train, disappears into the distance.

You swear and curse, because now you feel obliged to conjure up an excuse as to why you're late again. Then the whole day seems grey and irritating until you get home.

When you get home, once you've huffed and puffed and poured yourself a coffee or something stronger, you switch the TV or radio on.

Then and only then, when the unflappable News reader moves from nationally important things to locally important things, do you discover that the bus or train or river taxi that you missed, because you had to tie your shoe, crashed or sank leaving no survivors.

Then you think to yourself,

"Bugger! It's a good thing I wasn't on that."

Has that happened to you?

More than once or twice?

If you feel like you've cheated death on a regular basis, there is a very good chance that you have a Watcher.

Bob has a Watcher; his name is Irving and right now he should be teaching the recently divined Watchers, about the shivers and how to ensure their recently bonded humans enjoy a long and healthy life.

He should be doing that but he's not.

Right now, he's moving as fast as he can towards a dry, husky, sun bleached wheat field in the middle of the English countryside.

The shiver, which began as a tingle, was getting stronger and stronger and, knowing Bob, would not get better if Irving left him to his own devices.

Bob was shooting, although rationing had ended a few years ago; during the war, pigeons and rabbits had propped up the meat allowance and kept Bob and his family healthy.

He'd left the farm house three hours ago and headed for the small copse which acted as a green, shaded island in the middle of a tidal wheat and barley ocean. The tender breeze bending the, heavy eared, stalks into a whispering surf.

He'd sat on a coppiced stump and eaten the thickly breaded, thickly buttered, thickly gammon and mustarded sandwich constructed and wrapped in greaseproof paper by his mother.

That being done, he had waited for the gluttonous woodpigeons to rest in the tree tops in the midday sun, their pudgy wings barely able to lift their, grain swollen, body's.

Bob had bagged two with one shot, although he felt that he had probably only hit one of them.

The other one had probably died of shock when the, Russian made, double barrelled shotgun roared like Thor's hammer, tearing the tree tops into leafy confetti.

Both plump, feathered cadavers now lined the inside of a small, brown cloth sack which swung gently under the low branch.

Bob had moved away from the cooler refuge of the copse and was slowly ambling along one of the rows of wheat, which still stood defiant against the harvest.

He had watched the combine harvester as it had crawled up and down the field, combing the stalks at one end then, like Sweeney Todd, dumping the de-grained carcasses out of a trap door at the other.

He had watched until the field was about a quarter reaped, which was when the rabbits started running.

The rabbits in the field had warrens burrowed at the edges near the foot of the hedgerows.

Suddenly startled by the noise of the advancing machinery and disoriented by the drastic change in scenery. They made a break from the still standing wheat and bolted toward the drainage ditch which marked the boundary on one side of the field.

The harvester processed four rows in a single pass, so Bob made his way along the fifth, his gun cracked but loaded in readiness.

Irving moved fast across the open ground, a shadow-less heat shimmer on the edge of visibility, gliding over the ground towards the distant figure.

He knew what was going to happen, he had seen it, as the shiver had increased in magnitude, the impression had grown clearer.

He knew that Bob would raise the gun and take aim at a bolting rabbit.

The sudden change to his centre of gravity and the speed of his pivot would unbalance Bob and tip him into the path and jaws of the death machine, which had been making its steady approach behind him.

Bob would die and Irving would fade.

Irving pushed on, using more and more precious energy,

"This is going to be close." Irving thought, planning his intervention as he sped through the dry, wheat chaffed air.

He could see the rabbit, cowering between the stalks; it's life force glowing like a beacon, fear amplifying its' energy aura amongst a big and small polka dot jumble of life, this was it.

Irving let go, he'd balled up enough energy to fling a pebble at the rabbit, the stung rabbit leapt early and broke cover half a second before Irving's premonition.

Half a second early, Bob cocked and raised the twin barrels in a swift, easy action to lead the flash of brown, scurrying fur.

Irving looked on as Bob twisted and began to topple, the barrels pointed at the heavens as Bob's jacket was caught by the tines on the rotating wheel of the passing harvester, pulling him back into the wheel arch.

Both barrels roared into the sky, spitting lead shot in an angry salvo at the sun.

The tine bit into the jacket harder, pulling Bob's sleeves tight over his head and the gun held vertically against his body as he was twisted backwards, over the wheel like a tumbler at the circus.

The gun barrels gave way and contorted to fit the curvature of the wheel arch, in which Bob was a warped question mark.

His head was about to begin the downward journey under the wheel, to certain death and instant burial.

"Don't let it hurt." He thought, as his ribs cracked and broke, human anatomy losing its brief battle against physics, then with a judder everything stopped.

There was a metallic 'Twang' as the tine released its hold on Bobs jacket, allowing him to fall out of the wheel arch and flatten a patch of un-mown wheat beside the silent machine.

"What the bloody hell you doin' down there boy?" The farmer stepped off the driver's platform of the open top combine harvester, landing heavily on the dusty soil, before bending over to stand Bob up by his armpits.

"I was about to shoot that rabbit for the pot, I think I lost my footing and got caught up on the reel." Explained Bob, wincing at the sharp pang of a broken rib.

"Best get you to the doctors," The farmer smoothed his hair back, replaced his cap then brought a pipe out of his jacket pocket which he lit with a match, "don't look like you'll be shootin' much more anyhow, less it's around a corner." He gestured to the semi-circular curvature of the gun barrels.

Bob pressed, winced then pressed again at the broken rib, almost convinced it would just be bruised if he pressed it enough times,

"Thank you Mister Orton, best get those woodpigeons or my Mum will gut me."

Farmer Orton puffed on the pipe.

"I'll be blowed," a cloud of blue grey smoke puffed out of the corner of his mouth, "half a second later and you'd be gone boy." He muttered under his breath before heading across the field toward the tractor to take the boy into the village.

Back in the field Irving felt drained, he'd used a lot of energy, probably more than he needed to, but at that range he had to be sure that the rabbit would move early.

"He'll be the fading of you Irving."

Another Watcher, Farmer Orton's Watcher, sat up on the driver's platform.

"Thanks 'You bastard Henry Orton, no more nookie for you', I owe you one."

Irving slumped down into the field and rested.

A brief history of Watchers:

As you may have guessed by now, Watchers are not human.

Their evolution, however, is closely linked to that of modern Homo Sapiens.

They exist, in our world, as an energy field, on the edge of the visible spectrum.

Their beginnings, in the dark ages, were as parasites feeding off human hosts, leeching life energy until there was no more.

The practise of leeching which prolonged their existence led to fear, folk law and most notably, tales of Vampires and Ghouls who drank their prey to death.

The Watchers continued to thrive alongside humans until the spread of Bubonic Plague, which wiped out great swathes of people, rats and Watchers across Europe in the middle ages.

This led the Watchers to have a meeting of the elders, and ultimately the creation of 'The Promise'.

'The Promise' is an agreement that each Watcher, at its divining, will be bound to one human which it will watch over to prevent it from dying.

In exchange the Watcher will draw enough energy from its bound human, to sustain and ultimately divine its self, some Watchers rejected 'The Promise' and continue to leech to this day.

The act of divining is how the Watchers reproduce.

Much like an amoeba the Watcher stores energy throughout its life then, usually at the end of its bond with the human, it uses that energy to split into two, creating a newly divined Watcher who will be bonded to another human by its elder.

Incidentally, Watchers take their names from the first words they hear after their divining.

Irving's full name is 'Irving Berlin's Alexander's ragtime band', which, when Irving was divined, happened to be playing on the wireless next to the bed in which baby Bob had just been born. A moment sooner and he might have been called "I am pushing you bloody fool, why don't you do something useful!"

Bob finally drifted into a light sleep, his ribs bandage by the doctor who had prescribed the pills to lessen the pain and make him drowsy.

The shimmering presence of Irving settled nearby, waiting for Bob's sleep to become heavy before he could draw on Bob's energy to replenish his own, tomorrow he had a lecture to give.

The next morning Bob woke late, his mum had allowed him to sleep-in to help him fix quicker.

He felt like he'd been run over and although that was the case, he didn't feel like he'd slept at all.

The jagged lightning of pain shot out from his chest in all directions, making sure his toes, fingers and scalp were all aware that his ribs were still broken, and that yesterday's painkillers were no longer in his system.

Each breath rippled pain around his body as Bob tried to put on his trousers, using one hand and the least amount of movement possible.

Next came the shirt which, by the pained expressions and sucks of breath, fitted like an iron maiden.

Hobbling gently downstairs Bob paused briefly by the front door to examine the arch that his shotgun now described.

He was lucky to be alive, but Bob felt annoyed that he would now have to buy another shotgun.

He walked into the kitchen and was greeted by a warm cup of milky tea, two chalky pills and a ham sandwich placed in front of him by his mum.

"Morning mischief," she smiled, "how are you feeling after your sleep?"

Bob slurped that he was "a bit sore," from behind his favourite Bovril mug.

"Well, your Dad's up the top field if you're feeling up to it." His mum announced over her shoulder as she filled the deep stone basin with hot water and soap flakes.

Irving was miles away, at the Library, in the town that served as a service hub for the surrounding villages and hamlets.

He and the new Watchers were in the corner of the Library building and while the business of checking books in and out continued around and sometimes through them, the Library's human contingent remained oblivious to Irving's lecture.

The group of Watchers were attentive and absorbed the instructions, hints and tips, which Irving had given them, in the way a conspirator would pass on a dastardly plan; it was a trick he had learnt from his diviner.

Take it away, just get rid of it! had stayed close to Irving when he was newly divined.

He'd shown Irving the ropes and shared 'secret' information to help Irving be a better Watcher.

Information which Irving had later learned was common knowledge but had held onto, even after Take it away had faded, because of the confidence it had given him.

This 'hidden' wisdom carried even more weight because, in the eyes of the newly divined Watchers, Irving was one of the best.

Everyone knew Irving and the Watcher's art he had been perfecting ever since he was bound to Bob.

Irving's outside-the-box interventions which had saved Bob on far too many occasions, had become legends that the elders would tell the newly divined.

Anecdotal tales of how Irving had saved Bob from drowning by manipulating a situation, where Bob would throw a sharpened stick into another boy's leg rather than take his turn on the rope swing. The rope would have snapped over the river and dumped Bob, head first, onto the stony riverbed breaking his neck.

Irving had dutifully answered the braver questions, which related to exaggerated versions of different solutions he had dreamt up to keep Bob's fat out of the fire.

"Why don't all humans have a Watcher?" The question came from You are Not calling our Son Billy the Kid.

Irving though for a second.

"There used to be loads of Watchers, more Watchers than humans once, but they weren't really the same as we are now." The group was focused on Irving's explanation.

"They weren't bound to one human, so they went around drawing from any human they wanted to."

"Like the Leechers." You'd better not be asleep Brian chipped in enthusiastically.

"Just like the Leechers," Irving agreed, "And when the human died, the Watcher drew from someone else."

"Why aren't there lots of Watchers then?" You are Not calling our Son Billy asked.

"A plague." Irving lowered his voice to a hiss, "The Black Death, they called it. During the Dark Times the humans got sick and most of them died." His voice turned into a low snarling growl for effect.

"The Watchers started fading too. Without humans to draw from, they started drawing from each other. They became Leechers." The new Watcher drew back instinctively, gripped by the described horror.

"It was too much," Irving said softly, "the leeching had to stop and the Watcher's knew something had to change."

"The Promise." The whole group muttered in unison.

"That's right, The Promise, you all spoke the words at your bonding. They're the same words that have been spoken by every Watcher from that day to this." The mood of the group had lifted again, "they're the same words which changed the world for humans and Watchers, they gave us all a future."

The Q & A was brought to an impromptu halt by a library member, who had unwittingly pulled a chair into the energy field of one of the new Watchers.

The resultant static shock was much to the amusement of the other Watchers.

Once Irving had regained control of the assembled group, he used what just happened as an example of the limitations the Watchers had in the human world.

"They cannot see us, they cannot hear us, and they cannot feel us," he gestured to the man who was rubbing his elbow.

"Aside from a mild electric shock, which we've all just witnessed, so you need to be inventive to keep your human alive."

Irving allowed a pause to help cement this information within the new Watchers.

"Remember, catch the shiver early and you may get a few more thinking seconds, ignore the shiver and you will fade." He left the solemnity of this last statement hanging before allowing the new Watchers to get off back to their newly bonded humans.

Back at the farm Bob pulled on his second boot, rubbed his ribs to make sure they were still broken, stepped out of the door and collided with his dad who was on his way into the farmhouse. Bob got back to his feet, winded by the pain in his chest.

"What are you doin' home?" his mum asked, from the kitchen doorway,

"You okay there lad?" his dad asked, resting a strong hand on Bob's back.

Bob straightened up as the pain subsided and nodded his reply as his dad hung his jacket on a peg.

"Greville died this afternoon," he announced, levering the heel of one Wellington boot off using the toe of the other, "doctor reckons he had a heart attack."

"Poor Virginia," him mum's concern for the recently widowed farmer's wife was genuine. Farmers, although competitors, were a tight knit community.

Bob's mum knew how lost she would feel, if her life were to be pulled from under her, by the death of her husband, "I'll take up a steak and ale pie tomorrow, see how she's doing."

Greville Orton's death seemed a bit surreal to Bob, he'd seen him yesterday, almost been run over by him yesterday.

He'd seemed alright, Bob wondered if almost running him over had weakened Greville Orton's heart to the point of killing him.

His mum must have sensed Bob's thoughts; she walked over and ruffled his hair,

"Greville had a funny heart for a long-time Bobby, it's a wonder he lived this long," she smiled and patted his shoulder, "we'll take Mrs Orton a pie up tomorrow, offer our condolences."

Irving drifted across the fields, through trees and over roads on his way back to the farm.

As he had expected, Bob had stayed out of trouble all day, he hadn't felt the slightest twinge of a shiver.

Which meant that Bob had been in bed dosed up on painkillers.

Or had felt so drowsy and weak, after Irving had drawn the energy out of him during the night, that he had rested up all afternoon.

The late summer sky was warm and noisy with bird song as they ushered in a bronzing sunset.

In the distance, Irving noticed the flicker of a blue light as he drifted over the summit of one of the gentle undulations, which rolled the fields into soft peaks and dips.

As Irving got closer he realised the blue light, that flared in the evening sky, was the beacon that crowned an ambulance.

It sat in the same field in which he had staved off Bob's death yesterday afternoon.

Irving could feel panic rising within, he felt for the shiver or a tingle which preceded the shiver, but there was nothing.

Satisfied that Bob hadn't gotten into any more trouble today, Irving headed for the ambulance.

The combine harvester had shorn two thirds of the field and now stood as a silhouette against the closing day, Irving looked on as a policeman and the ambulance driver shared a smoke.

The doors were closed behind the blanket shrouded body, which had been loaded into the back by two attendants.

The policeman, happy that there were no signs of foul play, had photographed the scene just in case. The local Doctor had noted a time of death.

All that remained was for the coroner to confirm the suspected cause of death was heart failure.

As Irving looked on, he heard his name,

"Irving." It was soft, almost a whisper, "Irving."

Irving turned.

"Irving, over here." It was You bastard Henry Orton, he was on the driver's platform and he was fading fast.

Irving moved up onto the platform, the haze of You bastard Henry was wavering; it looked like steam caught in a soap bubble.

"What happened You bastard Henry, what's going on?" Irving moved closer to the fading haze.

"A Leecher." Irving heard the words clearly as he watched his friend fade, he knew already but now there could be no mistake.

Only a Leecher would drain a Watcher to fading before draining the human to death, he would have to inform the elders.

Bob's X-ray

The next two weeks went by uneventfully for Bob; the broken bones in his chest, that kept him off work, would give him a dig occasionally and make him wince as they knitted themselves back together.

Bob had attended Greville Orton's funeral, he felt uncomfortable and awkward in the dark suit and starchy shirt.

He was surprised at just how many widowers and eligible bachelors were on hand to offer Mrs Orton their condolences and the offer of help should she need any.

The neighbouring farms had brought in Greville's last harvest, so Virginia Orton would be alright for money until next spring.

Then she would either make a go of it on her own or sell the farm to one of several speculative offers, which had already been made.

It was not so peaceful for Irving, although Bob had been recuperating and hadn't required the usual degree of supervision and intervention.

He had spoken with the council of elders about the revelation which had ultimately lead to You bastard Henry Orton fading in a field of wheat.

There was a Leecher amongst them.

The council had greeted the news with caution, suspicion and speculation,

"Are you sure You bastard said Leecher? "

"Why would a Leecher bother with such a small community of Watchers?"

"Maybe it was just passing through."

"Maybe You bastard and Greville were unlucky, wrong place at the wrong time, that sort of thing."

For the council, a Leecher was a big deal.

If they had to tell the community of Watchers that a Leecher had settled in the area it might cause panic and where there was panic, there was unrest.

Watchers took their eye off the ball when there was the threat of being devoured by a Leecher.

The Leecher would draw the energy from humans and Watchers alike and use the glut of life force to spawn more Leechers into the world.

'No' the council decided, this was probably a one off, a Leecher passing through, no need to cause panic unnecessarily.

Even He's as pink as a piglet Mary who was bonded to Leith Aitken the local butcher and More towels get more towels we've been blessed with twins, who watched Vicar Molyneux, agreed that starting a needless panic was not the way forward.

In fact, until there was reason to believe otherwise, the council would assume that the Leecher had gone and gave Irving strict instructions that there would be no more talk of a Leecher in the area. Irving had agreed, satisfied that the council were keeping an eye on things.

The following two weeks had seemed to confirm the council's assumption that the Leecher had been passing through.

Although the Watcher community had been a little on edge at the news of You bastard's fading, things soon fell back into their natural rhythm and with no more evidence of a Leecher the council of elders began to feel more at ease.

Irving tried to reassure himself that the Leecher had gone but the image of You bastard Henry fading into the hot evening air wouldn't leave him and didn't sit comfortably.

Something kept nagging at him right up to the day Bob went to have an X-ray taken of his mending ribs, to make sure there hadn't been any complications.

Irving had tagged along with Bob as he got on the bus which would trundle through neighbouring villages before heading into the City, where it would bully its way through narrow, cycle lined, streets with their honour guard of tall University buildings.

Bob was off the bus just before it hit the city centre, the large hospital stood like a Roman temple, crammed into the inner confines of the city's atmosphere for convenience, where it lay like a beached whale.

Irving moved in Bob's shadow, hospitals were full of opportunities for instant death or dismemberment.

It was only right that the place in which lives began as well as ended in equal measure should be filled with the mechanisms to efficiently facilitate both, Irving would have to be alert to every tingle and ready to act fast.

The journey to the X-ray department took Bob and Irving through the main doors of the hospital.

They passed a small kiosk that offered nothing the sick, dying or convalescing could ever want or need.

Passed departments that dealt with every area of the human anatomy, religious areas to deal with ailments of the spirit or immortal soul, and by rooms in which disease would be quantified in a simple chart or temperature measurement, terminal decline plotted on a graph.

The X-ray department was a few yards ahead on the left and as Bob and Irving neared the sign post, which pointed the way to X-ray, he was suddenly grabbed by the sound of his name being called, from the doorway on his right marked 'Chapel'.

"I thought it was you Robert." Father Molyneux let the chapel door swing slowly shut behind him.

"Oh, good afternoon Vicar." Bob responded, "just visiting I hope."

"Indeed Robert, I've been invited, by the hospital, to minister to the sick during the week, I was just about to start my rounds of the general wards, care to join me?" Father Molyneux sounded hopeful.

"Sorry Vicar, I've got an appointment." Bob gestured to the X-Ray sign opposite.

"Of course, of course," the Vicar sounded relieved, "how are the ribs?"

"Feeling a lot better thank you." Bob smiled, although he liked Father Molyneux well enough, something about the holy man's slightly nervous personality made him uncomfortable, he was glad to make his excuses and let the Vicar get on with his rounds.

The X-Ray department was almost empty.

Bob sat in a stiff-backed chair and waited his turn.

After a man dressed in paint spotted overalls, with his arm wrapped in a tea towel, and a lady in a green summer dress, sporting a swollen and purple ankle, took their turn in the lead lined room, the latter being wheeled around by an over attentive porter.

Bob was called.

Irving waited at the door of the X-Ray room while Bob sat on the bed, swung his legs around and had his chest targeted by the assistant radiologist.

X-Ray's had been found to have a strange effect on the Watchers, making them disoriented and clumsy.

Through the wired safety glass of the heavy blue doors, which marked the boundary of the X-Ray department, Irving watched as Father Molyneux strolled out of the chapel and made his way towards the general wards.

He was accompanied by his Watcher, and member of the local elder council, More Towels who gestured a salutation to Irving before moving through the corridor like the vicar's shadow.

Presently Bob re-emerged from the room, which to Irving still crackled and spat like chip fat as the residual radiation gradually faded.

The receptionist flicked through the notes on Bob's hospital file and, after reading the various annotated scrawls in a mumbled half-language, requested that Bob go to outpatients and wait to be seen.

Irving was back on the clock, weaving through the maelstrom of pedestrians, wheelchairs and wheeled beds that formed the bilateral flow in the hospital corridor, ever alert for stray syringes or scalpels, which might cut his bond short.

The onset of early afternoon had swelled the hospital population, filling the arterial corridors with families and friends, bearing bags of grapes, newspapers and other distractions to fill the time while the sick waited to get better or die.

The hospital air was tainted with disinfectant.

Bob wondered what the germs thought to it all, did they mind that they were the targets of a whole industry, focused on their systematic demise?

It made him doubt the accepted notion of evolution.

"After millions of years of evolution why haven't viruses evolved to make you feel better, fitter or stronger, rather than making you feel sick or killing you?" Bob had asked his Science teacher who had, after some silent contemplation, sent him to the headmaster's office for being insolent. The headmaster, who didn't understand why Robert was standing in his office, made a show of punishing him with a week of leaf duty and presented him with a besom broom, with which to sweep the leaves into a pile.

The week had been one of Bob's best, he had found a dead rat near the groundsman's shed, the dead rat would later be deposited in the science teacher's chalk draw causing uproar and elevating Bob's standing with the other pupils enormously.

He also made friends with the groundsman, who gave Bob a key to the shed, so he could light the small wood stove and put a brew on before starting his day of leaf patrol. The groundsman showed Bob how to set snares for rabbits and fashion a rudimentary crossbow, which Bob would later state were the only useful things he'd learnt at grammar school.

On the opposite side of the corridor Bob's attention was drawn to a doctor running toward him before disappearing into a doorway signposted as 'Neonatal' closely followed by two nurses.

As Bob neared the door he could see a flurry of activity as people and equipment were moved from one location to another.

One of the occupants of the ward backed out of the room into which everyone else seemed to be going.

Bob recognised Father Molyneux wringing his hands together as he backed further away from the door before turning and heading quickly for the exit,

"Are you okay Vicar?" Bob asked, as a visibly shaken Father Molyneux stumbled into the main corridor.

"Oh my, dear little mites, Oh my dear." The Vicar looked up at Bob before recognising him as one of his parishioners, "Oh, hello Robert, I'm afraid I might need to sit down."

Bob caught the vicar mid-faint; he persuaded a slumped Father Molyneux into an empty wheel chair that had been parked, through preparation or laziness, at the entrance to the Neonatal ward.

As Bob waited for the Vicar to regain consciousness, Irving suddenly became aware that More towels was not with Father Molyneux.

He looked closely at the vicar's neck, sure enough two pale yellowing pock marks began to spread out from the area where the energy had been hurriedly extracted.

Irving peered into the ward, then down at Bob before making his decision.

He moved through the wall into the nurse's station on the other side, then through the next wall from which he emerged into the reception desk.

The desk lamp popped as the bulb's filament gave under the dramatic increase of energy, it found itself exposed to, at the centre of the field which was Irving.

In a room, across from the reception desk, Irving could see doctors and nurses attempting to infuse life back into the two pale bodies who lay, motionless in see-through plastic cases next to each other.

Irving could already see that the spark of life had been extinguished, stolen by one of his kind.

He approached the room slowly, wary of the Leecher that could still be an occupant, through the wall at the corner.

When Irving was satisfied that, apart from all the human activity that was oblivious to his presence, the room was empty, he scanned for signs of More towels.

At that moment, More towels burst into the room from the opposite wall.

It was so sudden Irving had to stop himself from acting on instinct and vaporising the Watcher, whose arrival had taken him by surprise.

"Thank God, Irving, have you seen Peter?" More towels sounded frantic,

"Peter?" Irving was still spinning from the sudden arrival of the other Watcher and the realization that he'd almost blown him into the ether.

"Father Molyneux, Father Peter Molyneux." More towels sounded almost irritated by Irving's confusion.

"Oh, yes. Yes, Bob's with him, just outside the ward, what happened here?" Irving replied, regaining some of his composure.

More towels moved across the room, past Irving and through the door towards the corridor where Irving had left Bob and Father Molyneux.

Both Watchers stood back while the passing nurse, who Bob had flagged down, checked Father Molyneux over, advising him to have a sit down and a sugary cup of tea before doing anything else.

"It was a Leecher Irving," More towels explained, "he was draining the babies when Father Molyneux went into the room, managed to draw from Peter before I knew what was going on.

I went after him but I couldn't keep up, did you see him?"

"No, I saw the draw marks on Father Molyneux's neck and thought you might be in trouble." Irving replied.

More towels nodded his appreciation, "It's a shame I didn't get a good look at him then..." He paused to glance down at Father Molyneux, who was trying his best to convince everyone to stop making a fuss.

"Look Irving, you stay close to Bob, get him home as soon as you can, I'll make sure Father Molyneux gets some rest before I tell the elder council that we have a problem. There's no reason for us both to tell them the same things, especially as you didn't see anything, I can explain what you've told me. Unless there is something else you'd like to speak to them about?"

"No, it makes more sense if you tell them More towels, thanks, I'll get Bob home once he's done here." Irving was a little relieved that he didn't have to stand in front of the council again, so soon.

"Okay, I'll let you know if the council need to ask you any questions, and thanks for looking out for me. It's good to know you've got my back." More towels gestured his thanks to Irving then turned his attention to Father Molyneux who had been help back to his feet.

Bob handed back the Bible then stood back and allowed the vicar to dust himself off,

"You don't look so pale now Vicar." Bob observed,

"Thank you Robert, I'm not sure what came over me, I'm afraid I…" at that moment Father Molyneux's Bible slipped from his grasp, landing open on the floor in front of him like a leathery butterfly.

More towels flicked the thin pages over, with crackles of static, until he was satisfied with the selected chapter and verse.

The Vicar stooped down and picked it up, his fingers cradling the book's hinged spine and thumb separating the pages, which had opened when the book came to rest.

"Oh my…" Father Molyneux looked at the passage marked by his thumb, "Psalm one hundred and twenty-seven, verse two. 'It is in vain that you rise up early and go late to rest, eating the bread of anxious toil; for he gives to his beloved sleep.' Maybe I have been too zealous with my ministry of late, I think I may just take the rest of the afternoon as quiet contemplation."

"Good idea Vicar," Bob agreed, "I don't think God would envy you contemplating a small gin and tonic should the fancy take you." He smiled at the vicar and nodded, "I'd better be getting to outpatients before I miss my call, if you're sure you're okay?"

"Yes, I'm fine now thank you Robert, I might just make some enquiries into that gin and tonic you mentioned. Yes, yes."

The Vicar smoothed himself down, adjusted his collar and then, with a cheery wave, headed back towards the hospital chapel, leaving Bob and Irving to continue their journey to the outpatient's clinic.

For the rest of the day Irving stuck to Bob like glue, alert and ready to explode into action at the slightest sign of danger.

The visit to the hospital confirmed what Bob already felt from his ribs, they were healing nicely and what's more they could be left to their own devices.

The next few days saw Bob get back to normal around the farm.

The stalks from the wheat field had been baled ready for stacking and Bob set about piling them up with a pitch fork.

Gingerly at first then gradually growing in confidence that his ribs were not going to protest with the same vigour as they had a week ago.

His Dad had kept a close eye on him, in case he tried to do too much, occasionally advising him to "take a blow boy."

That evening, with the straw bales stacked neatly next to the barn, Bob hopped up onto the mudguard behind the driver's seat of the little blue, open topped Ford 3000, hanging on to the rim with one hand as his Dad traversed the ruts which described the well-used farm track.

Irving, who had stayed close to Bob all day, was relieved that there had been no more excitement. He moved along beside the tractor watching the clusters of glowing life force, which bunched up in preparation for the dark in burrows, sets, warrens and vast murmurations as starlings spilled, en masse, into the sky, pulsing as if a single entity.

As they neared the farmhouse, Bob could smell the crisp warmth of pastry as it slipped between the heavy punch of the diesel exhaust.

"Recon you're Mum's been baking a pie." His Dad smiled, gunning the tractor a little faster.   "Smells good." Bob agreed, "I hope she's made lots of gravy."

There was pie, and there was gravy, there was also a guest.

"The Vicar's here to see you Bob." His mum greeted him, by hand-combing his work stray hair into the semblance of a centre parting before she helped him take off his work jacket. "I've invited him to stay for dinner."

Bob's dad raised an eyebrow across at his mum, "It's a big pie." She mouthed before slapping him playfully across the top of his head.

Vicar Molyneux took his place at the table,

"For what we about to receive may the lord make us truly thankful." It was a quick grace but father Molyneux could sense the impatience in both Bob and his father. "I wanted to thank you Robert, for being a Good Samaritan at the hospital last week." The Vicar expressed his gratitude between mouthfuls of pie, gravy and fresh vegetables.

"You're welcome Vicar." Bob's reply was polite, functional and did not encourage further conversation, Father Molyneux ploughed on regardless.

In the kitchen, More towels and Irving stood, partially in the oven, so they could watch the meal proceeding in the other room while they talked.

"The other Elders are worried Irving." More towels sounded worried as well, "they're going to call a general meeting to let everyone know there is a Leecher amongst us."

"Won't that cause panic?" Irving asked, knowing the council's concerns about rattling the community unnecessarily.

"They, which is to say we, don't see how we can leave everyone in the dark when we are all potentially at risk." More towels looked through at the vicar in the next room, "I could have been faded Irving, like You bastard Henry."

"I haven't seen you in the congregation at Sunday service recently." Father Molyneux looked up between mouthfuls of steamed cauliflower that had sopped up some of the meaty gravy.

Bob's father shifted uncomfortably in his chair, but it was Bob who replied, "I haven't been in the congregation Vicar, so it would be surprising if you had."

A look of disappointment descended from Father Molyneux's wrinkled forehead, pulling his face into a frown, "I'm sorry to hear that Robert, may I ask why?"

Bob finished his mouthful before answering.

"Well, Vicar, I haven't been at church for the same reason that you haven't been seen at the synagogue recently." Bob smiled into the small pool of gravy as the disappointment on the Vicar's face changed to one of bewildered confusion.

"But I'm not Jewish Robert, I don't subscribe to their faith." Bob looked up at the Vicar with a smile in his eyes.

"Uhhuh." The noise, which Bob uttered, came from the back of his throat and from deep inside his sinuses simultaneously but said enough for the Vicar to know he was beaten.

"Oh, I see Robert. Please remember that the door is always open."

"The council want to see you again Irving." In the kitchen, Irving and More towels continued their discussion, "I told them you hadn't seen anything but, as you've been present on both occasions, they want to be sure they aren't missing anything. Tomorrow afternoon around two?"

"Okay." Irving's tone suggested that it wasn't okay.

In the other room, Father Molyneux had suddenly realised that he was urgently needed back at the vicarage and was in the process of thanking Bob's Mum for the dinner.

She was in the process of coercing Bob's Dad into driving the vicar back into town, a job which he soon delegated to Bob with great satisfaction.

Bob had agreed to be taxi, on the proviso that he could use the Austin Devon the following week, and dutifully chauffeured the Vicar back to the rectory, through the clingy heat of the late summer evening.

That night, the rain, which had been building throughout the day, cleaned the dusty air and polished the grass leaving the world tasting fresh once again.

The Council

The climbing sun had warmed the muddy puddles, reducing them to patches of soggy parchment by the time Bob rose from a fitful night's sleep.

He was greeted with a fried egg, a thick slice of bread, a sandwich deftly wrapped in beige greaseproof paper and a wicker basket that, Bob knew, meant he would be picking wild berries after breakfast.

The cycle ride took Bob into the countryside proper, away from the villages that dotted around the edges of the city like piglets around a sow.

He set a slow but steady pace, pedalling the dark green Raleigh at just above dawdling speed, wrestling with gravity as he balanced defiantly.

Enjoying the bird song, from the hedgerows that straddled the grass verge beside the road, and watching the lone buzzard which corkscrewed higher and smaller on hidden thermals.

Bob could imagine he was the last human on the earth, with so little evidence of further existence other than himself and the soft clicks of his rear wheel turning.

Eventually the twenty-minute bike ride veered off the tarmac and onto a stony track, which trundled alongside a field of corn stubble before snaking into a distant wood, the wicker basket bounced and creaked in complaint as the bike was bucked between stones and ruts.

On the edge of the wood a corrugated tin shed stood sentinel against the seasons, that had flaked its paint and rusted its bolts.

Inside the shed was cool and dark, rods of light sticking through the roof where ever the rust had bitten through.

Bob sat his sandwiches on the small shelf, that had been set onto the end wall to provide a storage surface.

Small hooks had been screwed underneath as a provision for coats, hats or braced pheasants. Against the sidewall lay the 'A' frame of a small ladder, which Bob lifted out of the door, before wheeling his bike in.

With the ladder over one shoulder, and the basket hitched over the top of the 'A', Bob made his way along the edge of the wood, where the thicket of brambles twisted through the broken shade of the trees.

Finding a ripe blackberry, Bob popped it into his mouth and waited for the sweet burst of sharpness to tighten his cheeks.

"Hoo hoo, boooootiful!" He exclaimed, as the sour grimace subsided, the picking and occasional eating then commenced.

It was a slow, sometimes painful, process as the bramble vines fought to claw back their berries with rasping thorns as the ripest, most succulent, fruit was stripped by contorting fingers that threaded though the tangled labyrinth.

From deeper in the wood, a woodpecker rattled like a snare drum, ignored by squirrels that danced around the mossy floor in an earnest quest to find, eat or bury every nut the world had to offer.

The heat built gradually as mid-morning turned into late morning, midday then early afternoon. Stopping for lunch, Bob examined his haul between bites of bread, the basket was almost full, he would eat his sandwiches, drink the bottle of lemonade, which he had rustled from the pantry, then finish off filling the basket before heading home.

Bob wiped at the bread crumbs, which clung to the edges of his lips, with the back of his hand and was presented with the evidence, in the form of a rich purple stain from wrist to knuckle, which attested to his blackberry consumption.

Irving stood before the full council, the familiar figures, which made up the Local council, now flanked the greater District council and at their head, directly opposite Irving, was a representative from the Watcher National council.

He had been considering Irving, for the last five minutes, in complete silence, just staring, not moving, not saying a word.

Irving had said, "Hello." Followed by "Um, I'm Irving Berlin's Alexander's Ragtime Band."

An attempt to break the silence, and get things moving along, that was greeted with more silent staring.

Finally, the head of the District council, Are you alright Mortimer, gave a grumble then spoke,

"Thank you for coming Irving, let me introduce you to the council."

Are you alright Mortimer, then proceeded to name the members of the Local and District councils who surrounded Irving in a semicircle, around the edges of the Library Archive Room.

"And finally, as our representative from the National council, the Watcher who has been watching you intently for the last five minutes, may I introduce, My goodness me Grace his willy is tiny."

"Have I seen you before?" My goodness me Grace was now staring more intently at Irving.

"I'm not sure your honour, I don't think..." Irving was cut short by My goodness me Grace, who seemed to be talking right through him and directly to the wall behind.

It was so disconcerting Irving had turned around, to check that there was no one behind him.

"You look like I've seen you before, up to no good I shouldn't wonder."

Are you alright Mortimer took the reins once again, trying to steer the meeting back onto a constructive path.

"We need to ask you about your recent run-ins with the Leecher Irving, as we understand it you've been on the scene twice now." Irving began to answer the question but was becoming increasingly aware of a slight tingle down his left side, almost too faint to notice.

"Um, yes, well sort of yes." Irving tried to focus on the question, "I was too late to save You bastard Henry Orton no more nookie for you, the Leecher had been and gone before I got there." Irving was slightly irritated at having to repeat himself, he had told all this to the Local council, all of who were now assembled around the edges of the venerable semicircle, at the first meeting. "I also didn't see the Leecher when he attacked Father Molyneux at the Hospital, More towels had chased him away before I got there, didn't you More towels?"

More towels, get more towels sat at the edge of the arc and looked embarrassed to be suddenly the centre of attention.

"Um yes, that is correct, the Leecher tried to leech from Father Molyneux before it realised I was there and then made its escape," More towels sounded flustered, "I gave chase but to no avail. I believe Irving arrived at the scene in time to see the Leecher flee."

"Is this the case Irving?" My goodness me Grace was staring at him again.

Irving stuttered, the tingle was gradually growing, slowly and slightly becoming more irritating, like a bee trapped in a tee shirt.

"Yeah... Yeah... Yes, well no, I mean I'm not sure, I mean I was there but I don't think I saw the Leecher, well maybe I did but didn't notice, I don't know." Irving blurted.

"Well which is it? Either you saw it or you didn't."

"I'm not sure your honour, I don't think I saw it either time."

"What other time? Have you seen it twice?" My goodness me Grace was becoming more energetic and had begun bobbing up and down like a cork at high tide.

"I don't think I've seen it at all." Irving protested, the tingle becoming a faint image in his mind's eye.

"Then why did you say you had seen it, are you wasting my time? Whom are you covering for?" My goodness me Grace, had started rocking backwards and forwards as well as bobbing up and down and looked like he might ping off into space at any moment.

"Irving has been at the scene on both occasions that the Leecher has interacted with Watchers, we thought it would be valuable to get his perspective on both occasions, as it might help us formulate a strategy." Are you alright Mortimer, held the reins again, "Now shall we begin once again? From the beginning if you would be so kind Irving."

Irving could see a faint flickering image.

44

Bob was laying on the ground; his face and arms were covered in blood and his eyes were closed.

Irving couldn't tell if he was moving and the tingle hadn't grown strong enough for Irving to see the cause, he would just have to wing it and hope for the best, again.

"I can't, I have to go, really, I have to go now. I'm sorry but I really have to go now." And Irving went.

Leaving Are you alright Mortimer, More towels, My goodness me Grace and the rest of the assembled council staring after him as he disappeared through the library wall.

Irving could see Bob's life force as a pinprick in the distance,

"This might well be the last of you Irving." He thought to himself, before refocusing on the speck that seemed to be a million miles away on the horizon, this would use a lot of energy and Irving was afraid, this time, he would be too late.

Bob surveyed the fortress of brambles that he'd stripped of berries earlier in the day.

He patrolled the outskirts looking for clusters of rich, ripe fruit to fill his basket.

He eventually settled for a clump of, berry heavy, brambles behind the initial stockade of thorny tendrils before, briefly, choosing the best angle of attack and means of infiltration.

The 'A' frame Orchard ladder was a triangular ladder tapered to a point at the top, supported by a single rear leg which was kicked out to form a tripod.

The rear, supporting, leg would not be required in his final sortie into the brambles.

He would lay the ladder onto the outer plants, using his weight to flatten a makeshift pathway to the glut of berries within.

The ladder was rested onto a thinner section of bushes.

Bob hooked the handle of the berry laden basket onto the crook of his elbow and began a slow traverse up and along the ladder, which lowered with every step.

He had ascended five rungs up the ladder before it, abruptly, stopped crushing the thorny plant and offered any hint of resistance.

The ladder had come to rest slightly off centre on a thick, heavily barbed stem that came from deep within the snarl of spiky leaves, and which stemmed a multitude of angry branches that clutched their treasured fruit with razor lined fingers.

Bob bounced, gently at first, testing the give of the wrist thick obstruction.

He bounced with more vigour, flexing the centre of the ladder before allowing the undulations to subside.

He would have to reposition the ladder away from the thick stem and try again.

He started to make his way back down the ladder.

Irving skimmed through cars, fences and startled livestock, which kicked out at the air and bleated hysterically as he made a beeline toward Bob.

The image of Bob, his face streaked with blood, had gained some substance in the minutes Irving had been travelling, although still not powerful enough to grant him the insight into the cause of Bob's impending circumstance.

The shiver was still weak.

Irving hoped this was because the cause of Bob's condition was a long way in the distant future, rather than being due to Bob's location being a long way from Irving.

Sparks crackled on the hinges of gates and across the heads of nails in fences as Irving's energy field sped through them with no regard to boundaries and feudal allotment.

Bob stepped back, the ladder bounced on the thick green stem, the undulation shifting the point of the ladder making it tilt and skew, he wobbled and fought to balance, the ladder shifted once more.

His arm instinctively waved the air like a tightrope walker, clawing back his centre of gravity, the basket slid along his forearm.

Bob's hand briefly forgot the circus act which was steadying him on the ladder and made a grab for the basket handle.

The ladder slipped sideways and threw him into the eager clutches of the vengeful blackberry tentacles.

They tore and slashed at his face and bare forearms, tearing through his shirt to rip at his chest and back, they clawed into his legs as he fell into a twisted mess.

The ladder, finding itself somewhat lighter, sprung up with a revitalised vigour and landed with a thud, neatly on the edge of the briar.

Bob lay still, deep amidst the twisted barbed vines; reports were coming in from all over his body, from slices that stung and gashes that had caused blood to pock mark his shirt.

"Death by a thousand cuts." He thought, trying to figure out which part of him would cause the least pain to move first.

The palm of his left hand was pressing into a large thorn; this would be first.

The raising of his left hand caused more thorns to bite into his elbow, the movement freed a stem which swiped across Bob's cheek, scoring a tiger claw-like wound just below his eye.

The image, now stronger, did nothing to slow Irving.

Although still some distance away Irving could now see that Bob was moving, the blood and wounds were clearer, the vision had more substance; the cause was pulling into focus as well.

Irving could see Bob bouncing astride the ladder, twisting and falling into the undergrowth.

As Irving tore over the fields, he had decided his course of action was to release a ball of energy, which would throw the ladder in the opposite direction and hopefully buy enough time for Bob to get off safely.

Bob had tested each of his limbs in turn; each one was trapped by the other, each movement causing incisions to be inflicted upon other areas of his body.

He would have to free himself, but it was going to hurt.

A lot.

Irving arrived too late.

As in his vision, Bob was lying in the middle of a tangled, twisted thicket of thorns and branches, his face, arms, legs and body striped with bloody scratches and deep slicing cuts.

Every movement was followed and curtailed by a groan or yelp of pain; Irving's planning was wasted.

He looked at the scene, it seemed futile, he couldn't help Bob now, he couldn't use his energy to part the bushes or even to cut one of the thinner stalks.

Irving felt deflated and useless and what was more, he had used a lot of energy to get here for nothing.

He sat amongst the bushes next to Bob and watched him tentatively move an arm or bend a leg against the sting of new wounds.

He had been sitting watching for a few minutes before the glare of the sun bounced and gleamed, drawing Irving's attention to Bob's trouser pocket.

"Bob's pocket knife!" Irving felt elated, his journey wasn't wasted after all, he just needed to get the pocket knife to within reach of Bob's thorn tethered hand. "Sorry Bob, this is going to hurt a little."

The small ball of energy built within Irving, he focused it into the top of Bob's thigh, the shock violent enough to jolt the leg upward in a spasm that freed the pocket knife, which Irving then encouraged towards Bob's raked fingers.

"Arrgouch!" The spasm had ripped his leg out of the clutches of green needles and into the gaping maw of others, new pain climbing on top of the old.

It was a few moments before Bob realised that his pocket knife was a few inches from his nose, a few moments later in was in his hand.

He began the slow process of freeing himself, cutting gingerly at first then making more assertive cuts, trimming the snaking vines away from his arms and head, eventually freeing his legs.

Finally standing within the bush, which had held him captive.

The bush was cut back into a rough path to Bob's freedom.

Most of the cuts had stopped bleeding by the time he stepped back into the sun shine where he took a minute to assess the damage to his clothes and skin.

The basket, which had fallen and toppled over, took a few moments to re-gather and fill with the berries which had spilled onto the grass that fringed the thorny bushes.

The cycle journey home was painful, the sun had dried the blood into scabs, which uncomfortably tightened and pulled at matted hair.

Early evening ushered Bob and Irving through the front gates of the farmhouse.

He wheeled his bike to the shed, propping it up on the stand that allowed it to slump, casually waiting.

Back in the house, Bob rested the basket of berries on the solid wooden table before making his way towards the bathroom.

"My good God, what happened to you?" Bob's mum was restocking the linen cupboard with fresh towels when Bob walked in.

"I fell into the blackberry bushes." Bob said as a matter of fact, he felt tired and just wanted to jump in the bath before crawling into his bed, "It looks worse than it is." He added.

"I should hope so, you look like you've been dragged through a hedge backwards!" his mum announced, "I'll call the nurse, you get yourself washed up."

Bob began to dispute the need for the district nurse to be called, but the look which he received from his mum, told him that the nurse would be called no matter what he thought.

Nurse Foot arrived twenty minutes later and greeted Bob, who had finished drying his hair, with a bottle of iodine and a handful of cotton swabs.

Ten minutes later, Bob's wounds had all been medicated, he looked like he was in the middle of an Iodine pox outbreak; smallish yellow brown dots covered him like a pink leopard.

The parts of him which had received deeper cuts had been dressed with a loose gauze, nurse Foot finished the treatment off by tying a thin piece of gauze in a bow around Bob's left thumb, she clipped the rough end of the dressing and flashed Bob a smile.

"That should help you stay out of trouble." She stood and brushed herself off before re-packing her bag.

"Um, thanks." Said Bob, a little uncertain of how to respond, "I'll try to."

"I recon she's sweet on you." Bob's mum teased as they watched the district nurse disappear down the road on her bike.

Bob woke early for work, he hadn't managed to shake the muggy tiredness which filled his head with, what felt like fog and socks.

His Grammar School education had led to an apprenticeship at Dix & Sons paper mill and print works.

Away from the farm, much to his father's dismay and his mother's delight.

Her observation that "Bobby's too bright to be a farmer," trumping any and all arguments his father had to offer on the subject.

The Iodine had faded a little, but not enough to prevent each scabby scratch from being the bull's-eye in a sandy blotch.

Bob jerked the bike off its stand and set off on the five-mile journey to the factory in the next village, Irving followed, feeling refreshed by the preceding nights replenishment but downcast by the knowledge that the council would expect an explanation.

"You look like one of them spotty dogs." Lesley Spencer was a proofer and had been adjusting one of the plates on the machine next to Bob's, "What you done to yourself Spotty dog?"

"Spence, have you nicked our spindle wrench again?"

Ray was a master printer, his parchment face and cracked hands looked as if they had been processed at the local tannery.

He had been shepherding Bob through his apprenticeship for the seven months Bob had been learning the trade.

"I'm just borrowin' it," Spencer replied, pulling the rollers into alignment.

"Why don't you use your own one? You're holdin' us up." Ray hadn't looked up from the work sheet he had been studying.

"Don't need to use mine 'cause I'm usin' yours." The roller was turned half a turn, then adjusted once more.

"Well give it back and bugger off so we can get on." Ray pinched the worksheet onto a clipboard which had been pinned, lopsided, onto a panel that covered the roller housing, then straightened to fill the six feet six inches, which his leathery frame occupied.

"Let's see if your spotty dog will get it," Les sneered before hurling the wrench towards a stack of spooled paper in the corner of the factory, "go on spotty dog, go fetch."

The thrum of the rollers steadily gathered pace drowned out Les's exaggerated laughter as Bob went in search of the spanner.

The print works was a daily nightmare for Irving, the spinning rollers, the heavy spools of paper and the toxic ink which stood in stacked barrels.

Any of it could cause the end of both Irving and Bob. A quick, flat, inky end.

Bob, the spindle wrench back in its place within the rank of tools on the metal shelving unit, set the plates and threaded the paper from the spool through the rollers.

He spun the machine up to complete a test run, checking the colour and print alignment.

Confident that the pigment recipe, measured in fractions of coffee tins, had been followed and was correct; Bob went in search of jump leads and vengeance.

The factory quietened as machines slowed and came to a halt, their hum replaced by the murmur of a lunchtime workforce.

Bob placed the spindle wrench, which he had used to sabotage the print alignment of the neighbouring machine, back on the shelf.

Clipping the jaws of the borrowed jump leads to the metal shelving, from the twelve-volt battery that he had hidden beneath a small upturned wooden crate, before heading off for his lunch.

Talk of the test match, weekend arrangements and anecdotes of tarts, cwumpet and missed opportunities bounced around the canteen like a tidal wash, until the scrape of wooden chairs against parquet flooring signalled the end of the lunch hour.

A small group containing Bob filtered back to the factory, in no hurry to get out of the lazy sun which still held court high in the sky.

"Right Wally, Dad says I can use the Austin, so we can go and get that Triumph of yours Saturday morning." Wally was a few years older than Bob and was about to buy his first car, a Lichfield Green, Mark 1, Triumph Spitfire.

A problem had arisen in getting to the Triumph showroom twenty-five miles away.

His Dad had refused to lend him the car or give him a lift to the showroom on what he deemed to be,

"A despicable waste of money."

Money which Bob was more than happy to see him waste, so long as he got to be a passenger occasionally.

The warmth of the sun was subdued inside the factory, the heat mixing with the stale, oily air with its tinge of sweat and cigarette smoke.

From the far end of the factory, where Bob and Ray worked, the relative tranquillity of resting behemoths was pierced by a sudden but continuous, chattering shriek that evolved into a spectrum of curses and blasphemies directed at Bob.

As they rounded the corner of the press, before it sent the ribbon of freshly printed envelopes or headed paper to the various cutting machines, both Ray and Bob were greeted by the sight of Les Spencer gripping the spindle wrench in, what appeared to be, a demonstration of ultimate effort.

The determination sending sharp spasms along his rigid arms and legs.

"You bloody basstarrd!" Les grimaced at Bob.

"Mind yourself Spencer," Ray laughed, brandishing the cut down broomstick that stirred the ink, "I reckon this dog bites."

He moved the box which concealed the car battery and disconnected one of the jump leads, with a sharp tap of the inky stick and burst of yellow sparks.

Les dropped the wrench and crumpled backwards, his muscles refusing to carry on unaided.

A dark damp patch spread across the front of his trousers as proof of the tension and sudden relaxation of all his muscles.

Les snarled up at Bob from the floor,

"Bob, you F." The hum and clatter of once dormant machines, now revived and pressed back into service, rolled over the rest of Les's profanity.

He got to his feet and waddled off in the direction of the manager's office.

Ray laughed as he replaced the mixing stick,

"Nice one boy," he smiled, "best you get this lot cleared up." Nodding his head in the direction of the leads and battery.

Bob said nothing as he looped the wire around his forearm, carrying the battery back out towards the yard, his satisfaction evident as a slight smile.

Early afternoon turned into late afternoon, the sun continuing it's decent in earnest, three rapid bursts of bell strikes signalled the end of the working day.

Cleaned rollers, oiled mechanisms and spooled paper slowed down and came to rest, allowing serenity to settle on the factory floor like the motes of microscopic confetti that softened the air.

In the yard, Wally caught up with Bob, Irving following like a cautious shadow.

"So, you'll pick me up Saturday mornin' Bob, what sorta time d'ya reckon?" Wally crabbed along beside Bob, his feet choreographed in a chaotic dance routine.

"Bright and squirrely Wally, you'd best be up on time."

Bob had waited for Wally on a few occasions and knew that, without fail, he would have to wait for him to get ready on Saturday morning.

Furthermore, Wally would have to wash, clean his teeth and put on fresh clothes before Wally's Mum would deem him fit for public consumption and allow him to leave the house.

Wally, like three fifths of the population, didn't have a Watcher and therefore stumbled and bumped through life on an unseen knife edge, their future left entirely to chance.

His association with Bob had, on occasion, been beneficial by proxy.

Irving's intervention in Bob's routine brushes with death, increasing Wally's longevity as a kind of knock on effect.

That, in addition to his refusal to willingly partake in his own personal hygiene, which seemed to keep people, and therefore danger, at a reasonable distance.

The ride home was uneventful, Irving had almost forgotten about the council, the Leecher and the difficult situation which he found himself in.

The setting sun bathing both Irving and Bob with a feeling of carefree invincibility.

Bob freewheeled into the farmyard, his shoes scuffing the dusty mud into small plumes that chased him as he slowed to a halt outside the small outhouse where he stowed his bike.

Inside the farmhouse, the air felt much softer, Bob placed his green satchel next to the shoe rack that stood sentinel under the row of brass coat hooks.

Through the window which opened onto the back of the house, Bob could see his mother in a slightly stooped, semi run, brandishing a shallow bowl of grain.

Lucy had escaped again.

Bob stepped back out into the sunlight, the backyard a cacophony of real and faux chicken noise. Lucy was one of the resident chickens who provided the farm with eggs to either eat or sell and, like the other chicken, was given free range of the farm yard to scratch up bugs and grubs from dawn until dusk.

Unlike the other chickens, Lucy was not fond of her PM curfew.

She would dodge, charge and weave, trying to escape capture and every evening Bob's mother would be drawn into a battle of wits with a small brown bantam.

Until Bob arrived home and coaxed the little bird back into the safety of the coop.

As it happened, Bob's presence had little to no effect on the chicken but Irving's presence mesmerised Lucy, as it would all chickens.

They could sense the Watchers but not really see them, leaving the chicken brain a little confused, rendering the chicken immobile as it pondered the conundrum it had been presented with.

To onlookers it appeared that Bob, the chicken whisperer, had a calming effect on the chickens and therefore ultimate power over all poultry.

There had been no contact from the Council, which was both a relief for Irving and at the same time a little unsettling. He knew something must be on the cards.

Some sort of punishment or reprimand from the Council for leaving their audience in the way that he had.

Meanwhile, the peace had been wonderful and allowed him to concentrate on keeping Bob out of trouble.

The subsequent Tuesday and Wednesday had been quiet, Irving had gone to work with Bob at the print works, making sure he didn't fall into any machinery or ingest any toxic chemicals.

For his part, Bob had managed to keep himself clear of trouble, news of the prank on Les had bounced around the factory and kept Les out of his way.

By Thursday Bob's iodine blotches had all but faded, leaving only the deepest of scratches as proof of Bob's tangle with the Blackberry bush.

It was Thursday afternoon when Irving received word from the Council that he was required once again, this time he would also have to account for his actions during the last meeting.

More towels had conveyed the news to Irving that the council was not impressed.

"My goodness me Grace is suspicious Irving. The council thinks that maybe you are covering for the Leecher." More towels continued before Irving could interrupt with his innocence, "I know Irving, I know, but you have to understand how it looked when you ran out of the meeting without answering the Councils questions. Not good Irving, that's how it looked." Irving thought about his predicament for a few seconds.

"So, what should I do?" He asked, confused about the revelation and what it would mean for him.

"Well," began More towels, "I suggest you stay for the whole of the meeting and answer their questions as honestly as you can."

"What about Bob?" Irving asked, "the meeting is on Saturday morning and Bob is going to pick up a car with his friend."

More towels thought for a while, "I'm not going to tell you how best to watch your human Irving, but if you leave two meetings you have got to admit it's going to put you in the spotlight, don't you think?"

Irving had to admit that More towels was right, he would need to get through this meeting as quickly as possible and hope they didn't ask too many questions.

As Saturday drew closer Wally grew more and more excited about driving his new car, he had checked, double, even triple checked that Bob was still able to give him a lift to the car show room. Everyone in the print works canteen had been informed, to some degree, that Wally was picking up his brand-new Triumph Spitfire on Saturday.

On Friday evening, after work, Bob helped his Mum wash the blackberries and pull out the stalks ready for crushing, there were measured jugs of sugar surrounded by an army of empty jam jars amassed on the kitchen table, lined up and ready for the big push.

Irving had settled himself in one corner of the kitchen, it felt like the calm before the storm, although there was no way to know how the council would approach the meeting.

Although he figured that it was a safe bet My goodness me Grace was going to be more hostile than their first encounter.

He had decided that he would take charge of the meeting to speed up the interrogation and avoid any merry-go-round questioning.

Irving's certainty had bought with it a cool composure which allowed him to settle back and watch the jam making process which was going on around him.

Saturday morning arrived.

Undead

Bob was awake bright and early, he had fed the chickens, collected the eggs and washed the car in preparation for the inspection his father would carry out before Bob was entrusted with the keys.

He had sat down and eaten breakfast, at the kitchen table with his mother and father before dusting of his shoes and giving them a quick polish.

Then, cap on head, driven the six miles to Wally's house for the long wait he had already resigned himself to.

He wasn't disappointed, Wally was still sound asleep when Bob rapped on the door.

"He's not up yet Bobby, lazy tyke's been called three times, I took him a cup of tea up an hour ago, he's drunk that and gone back to sleep." Wally's Mum commiserated with Bob, offering him a cup of tea or coffee and the opportunity to turn him out of bed.

Bob politely declined the drink but took up the second offer and headed up the skinny stairs to animate a sleeping Wally.

The bed covers were thrown back and a glass of water, which Bob had spotted on the cabinet beside the bed, was dumped onto the head of the sleeping boy.

Wally sprung up with a look of anger and confusion, startled by Bob's presence and by the rude awakening,

"What the bloody hell Bob?" The anger subsided slightly once Wally had recognised Bob, but was quickly replaced with confusion, making Wally mildly annoyed but very confused.

"Up you get Wally, time to go get your car, unless you've changed your mind?" A smile slowly spread across Wally's face as his brain joined the dots, until finally he was grinning at Bob.

"Right you are Bob, give us a minute." And he was up, pyjama's being discarded onto the hallway floor as Wally made his way into the bathroom to carry out the briefest of washing routines.

Bob went back out and waited in the Austin Devon, keeping the engine idling in the fresh morning air.

Irving was waiting for the council to convene, he had arrived at the library almost an hour ago and watched the members of the District and National Councils move through the wall into the archive room, in which he had been interviewed last week.

The room was in the process of being mopped by the janitor who, oblivious to the other occupants, wondered why he kept getting static shocks.

Finally, Irving was called in, the group was smaller this time, he noticed that none of the local council were present.

In fact, most of the district council weren't there either, Irving began to feel a little unsettled.

The Austin Devon threaded along the twisted, knotted country roads as Wally pointed directions to Bob who, having never been to the car dealership before, was driving blind.

The presence of the road atlas his father insisted accompanied the car at all times, providing him with some comfort should they get lost.

Irving had been introduced to the members of the reduced investigating council, which seemed to be headed by Are you alright Mortimer and flanked, once again, by My goodness me Grace.

"I guess you're wondering why this is a much smaller assembly Irving?" It was a rhetorical question which Are you alright Mortimer proceeded to answer immediately, "The council believes that the Leecher has, somehow, infiltrated our ranks and is being passed information by one of our own community." My goodness me Grace stared at Irving hard.

"A spy, in the council?" Irving asked, genuinely puzzled by the revelation as well as the line of questioning.

"We believe it has a sympathiser," My goodness me Grace barked, "passing on information."

Are you alright Mortimer pressed on,

"Would you explain why you left the last meeting in such a hurry Irving?" Irving began to explain the circumstances surrounding his exit during the last meeting.

They were lost.

Wally's directions had run out.

Bob pulled over near a small village road sign which showed the miles and general direction of various nearby towns and villages as well as London.

"So, what's the address of the dealership?" Bob asked, flicking through the pages of the Austin road atlas and touring guide of Great Britain, second edition.

"I don't know." Wally replied, "How am I supposed to know that? I've only been there once."

"Your appointment letter Wally, the address will be on the letter confirming your appointment." Wally looked at Bob blankly, then started fishing around in his trouser pockets until a crumpled crust of paper appeared from his back pocket like a failed magic trick.

He unwrinkled the paper and smoothed it out on his trouser leg, noticing a patch of spilt jam near his right knee in the process.

The address was in the corner and Bob started cross-referencing the address against the index of the road atlas, before flicking to the relevant pages, while Wally tried to remove the jam stain from his trousers, using some spit and his thumbnail.

Then they were on their way again, Bob turning the car in the road to face the way they had just come.

Irving stayed calm. The questions were repetitive, just turned and reworded slightly, he wondered if they were trying to catch him out, whether they thought he was the informant, or even the Leecher.

"Bob had already fallen into the bushes when I arrived." Irving answered the question again, "I helped Bob free himself, then I followed him home. I've told you this."

After what felt like an eternal pause, Are you alright Mortimer mumbled quickly to My goodness me Grace before addressing Irving,

"After you left the meeting Irving, the Leecher struck again."

"It drew Miss Carmichael, the piano teacher, to death and faded This is the BBC World Service, while you were 'helping your human'." My goodness me Grace announced sharply.

Irving was stunned.

"I didn't know, I didn't know This is the BBC World Service, I mean we'd met. You don't think that I..." Irving stumbled over his words, "I wouldn't, I couldn't do that, I was helping Bob."

My goodness me Grace sneered,

"We only have your word for that, don't we Irving?" It was this remark, this distrust that suddenly lit the fires within Irving.

"Look, if you don't believe me then stop asking these stupid questions and get to it, because believe me or not this is a waste of my time." Irving was angry.

Bob turned the Austin onto the forecourt of the dealership, parking in a wedge of shade to keep the car cool for the journey home.

The engine wound down and died with a judder.

Bob turned the key and, once removed, tucked it deep into his trouser pocket.

Wally bounded into the office, with Bob bringing up the rear, and caught the eye of one of the salesmen, who was looking busy behind a sturdy wooden desk.

"I've come for my car." Wally called excitedly from across the office space.

The salesman finished the paperwork he had been completing, stood up and ushered Wally and Bob to matching, upholstered chairs before taking Wally's details and cross-referencing against the main diary.

There were forms to sign,

"Here, here and here."

"And here."

Wally removed an envelope from inside his shirt and counted out the money in front of the salesman who counted it himself then signed a chit, which he passed to Wally, taking the envelope full of money to a back office, to be counted for a third time before being promptly placed in the safe.

The purchasing documents were signed, by both parties, and the vehicle log book request form was given to Wally to complete while the salesman went to get the car brought round to the front.

He returned with a shiny set of keys in his hand.

Wally had a problem.

Are you alright Mortimer tried to calm Irving down,

"Nobody is suggesting you've done anything wrong Irving, we just need to gather as many facts as we can, so we can pin point exactly where this Leecher is hiding."

The janitor, who had been mopping the floor in even, rhythmic sweeps, passed through two of the assembled council, letting out a shrill yelp as pins of electricity pricked at his arms.

"And it seems like you've been at the centre of everything." My goodness me Grace chimed in.

"Can you take us through each incident, step by step, just in case we've missed something, some valuable clue." Are you alright Mortimer asked.

"Fine." Replied Irving, resigning himself to the realisation that this meeting was going to go on, maybe forever. "I was tutoring the new Watchers in the dark arts of keeping their human alive when I got the first tingle." He went over events once again, knowing there would be no valuable clue because the council had been told everything that had happened, several times.

Wally had forgotten to bring his driving licence, he had checked every pocket in his trousers and shirt to no avail, they had even checked the car to make sure wally hadn't dropped in down the side of the seat.

"I can't let you take the car off the forecourt unless all the forms are completed." The salesman was not going to budge, no matter how much Wally protested, "And without your Drivers Licence number just there," he indicated a segmented box on the top right corner of one of the forms, "you can't complete the forms, can you?"

It seemed like a lost cause, Wally had thrust his hands deep into his pockets and had decided to sulk. Bob looked at the form.

"Why do you need Wally's Drivers Licence number?" he asked, still looking over the form to make sure there was nothing he had missed.

"It says there, 'To be completed by the driver of the vehicle' it's so in the event an accident on the way home, you'll be covered by the insurance underwriters." The salesman tapped his finger on the paper to further indicate the text he was reading.

"But why does it have to be Wally's Drivers Licence number? I mean, it says driver of the vehicle, not owner of the vehicle." The salesman was looking a little closer at the form as Bob continued, "So if I were to drive it back to Wally's you'd need my Drivers Licence number, wouldn't you?"

"Well, yes I suppose so." The salesman conceded, then asked to see Bob's drivers licence.

The form was filled in, much to Wally's enthusiasm, before the salesman went away to collect the showroom manager.

"It's lucky you brought your Licence with you Bob, otherwise we'd have been stuck." Wally exclaimed, patting Bob's shoulder.

"You just be careful in the Austin Wally, you scratch it and, once my Dad has had my guts for garters, he'll be coming for yours." Bob warned, not so sure that he had made the right decision after all.

The manager came out of his office with the salesman, shook Bob and Wally by the hand, handed over the keys to Wally before returning to his office.

Irving felt a tingle, he had been running through the events in the hospital when the Leecher attacked Father Molyneux.

There was a faint image, which briefly flashed in Irving's consciousness, like the after image of a photograph in a thunderstorm, the tingle grew and began to distract Irving from the questions and from his answers.

"So, after you left Bob with Father Molyneux and decided to confront the Leecher, what did you plan to do when you met him?" Are you alright Mortimer asked, encouraging Irving to walk through him memory of events, step by step.

"I'm not sure I had a plan," Irving replied, the tingle was growing, "I just had to help... help um..."

"Yes Irving?" Are you alright Mortimer tried to more Irving along, "You just had to help."

"Sorry, yes, I just had to help More towels, I thought he might be in danger." Irving wanted the meeting to be over, the tingle was growing fast.

Again, the image flashed, this time clearer and for longer, Bob was laying on the ground.

"You burst in to the room with no plan and no idea of the location of the Leecher?" My goodness me Grace asked.

Irving decided he was not going to be led.

"I was concerned that More towels was in trouble, I don't suppose I needed a plan. It was a choice of help or do nothing, you weren't there so I couldn't ask you for your advice." He quipped, aiming his barbed reply directly at My goodness me Grace.

Bob and Wally circled the shiny green car, Wally popped the door open and sat in the seat experimentally bouncing to test the springs.

"I bet she goes." He exclaimed rolling the steering wheel from left to right and back.

"There is a complimentary gallon of four-star in the tank." Added the salesman.

"Right Wally, well let's fill her up so we can get going, okay?" The journey there combined with Wally's exuberance and complete lack of common sense was beginning to wear a little on Bob's nerves.

"Yeah, okay Bob, can we take the top down first?" Wally asked.

The salesman went through the procedure of unclipping the fabric fasteners from the hoodstick, and in which order to fold the hoodsticks down once the soft-top had been folded over the luggage compartment.

It took five minutes to show Wally how to take the soft-top down and how to put it back up again.

It took Wally fifteen minutes, and some prompting from the salesman, to successfully lower the fabric once more.

The dealership had a petrol station forecourt alongside it and Bob obligingly took the keys from Wally and idled the growling car to the nearest pump.

The attendant came out of the building and started pumping the "Five quid of four-star." Into the tank as Wally requested.

"Right Wally, you drive the Austin and I'll follow in the Triumph," Bob had sidled up to Wally while they watched the numbers spin around on the petrol pump, "when we get to the next village, you find somewhere to park up so we can swap over, take it nice and easy."

The attendant was paid for the fuel, Wally returned to Austin and Bob started the engine of the Triumph, which growled at him again, eager to roar at the wind.

Wally pulled onto the road,

"Right you are Wally." Bob indicated that he was ready to follow and pulled onto the road behind the Austin; they were on their way.

Bob was lying motionless in a field, there was no blood, but Irving could tell he was injured.

The tingle had become a shiver and the image had become more substantial.

It didn't reach back far enough for Irving to figure out the cause just yet, but he knew he would need to be closer and soon.

"When you left the last meeting Irving." Are you alright Mortimer had been talking to Irving while Irving had been concentrating on Bob's predicament, "where did you go when you left the last meeting?" Irving looked at Mortimer for a few seconds, thinking about the advice More towels had given him about not leaving the meeting and answering all the questions.

"I went to help Bob… I really am sorry about this and I know this must look bad, but I must go. Again"

Irving looked sheepishly along the line of councillors as he made his way towards the wall. "Once I'm done I'll pop back if that's okay."

Irving had crashed out of the meeting again and was speeding across the English countryside, with no idea of how he was going to pull Bob's fat out of the fire, he knew he had a long way to go.

The town was beginning to thin out, the houses stuttering in their placement, Wally had been right on the heavy end of the, thirty miles per hour, speed limit.

Bob had held back, hoping that Wally would slow down to match his speed.

But as the demarcation between thirty and national speed limit approached, Wally had accelerated to meet it.

By the time they passed the striped pole, with its white disk and black diagonal line, the Austin was doing sixty.

The Triumph easily matched it for pace and Bob found it difficult, now that he was on the winding country roads, not to push the accelerator pedal to the floor and allow the rasping rumble of the engine to engulf him.

The Austin was accelerating away from Bob again.

He encouraged the Triumph on, enjoying the speed but telling himself that he would have to give Wally a stiff clip around the ear when they stopped.

The speedometer told him that the Austin must be doing close to seventy miles per hour.

Bob had bounced off a tree and was lying motionless in a field, the precognition was filtering through slowly as Irving flew through houses, garden sheds and paddocks, almost oblivious to his surroundings, a blur in the ether.

He was aware that Bob was moving fast, it made pinpointing him difficult amongst the miasma of life.

Irving would make fine adjustments when he was closer, for the moment he just needed to get there in time.

The sky menaced with dark, swollen rain clouds that filled the air with the faint taste of lightning, the steadily condensing energy adding a fluorescent aura to the clouds above Irving.

He still didn't have enough information to start putting together a plan of action, the strength and speed at which the revelation was growing was not good, it meant that zero hour was rapidly getting closer.

The two cars flashed by a sign post which revealed that the approaching village was five miles away, the road swept around cambers and inclines, sporadically flanked by high verges, hedgerows and drainage ditches that kept the arable fields corralled away from the ribbon of tarmac.

Bob felt the first hint of rain touch his forehead, he would need to stop soon and put the top up before the clouds opened.

Ahead the road chicaned slightly before running up to a tight, almost ninety-degree right-hand bend, Bob cycled down through the gears with one hand as the other shimmied the car, first right then left, the engine whinnying down as the revolutions got less and less.

Irving was still miles away, he was now privy to the whole incident, both cause and effect. He could see the car leaving the road, he saw Bob hitting the tree and flopping onto the dirt, this was going to be close, again.

Bob watched the Austin disappear around the corner just as he exited the chicane, the Triumph had been reined back down to fifty as Bob positioned himself for the approach to the corner.

The Leecher had him.

He felt tired, very tired. As if all his energy had been sucked out of him.

He turned the steering wheel to the right before passing out, his upper body lolling forward and to the right, pulling the steering wheel further round.

Bob lifted his head, as the car hit the apex of the corner with the backend fighting for grip.

The rear tires caught and straightened the car, this time jolting the car and its passenger towards the grass verge which edged the road.

He noticed that Wally had stopped the Austin, in the middle of the road, a little way from the corner. As the front wheels hit the grass verge he wondered if, had he made the corner, he could have stopped the Triumph before it smashed into the back of the Austin.

The Spitfire was airborne; Bob could see the ripe clouds as he soared towards them, the car then bucked like a stallion as the rear wheels clipped the verge, throwing him into the air and into the stout trunk of a horse chestnut.

He had hit the tree with his chest, his legs pulling his body further round before kinetic energy released its grip and dumped him on the ground, his body slightly twisted onto his left side.

The car, once returned to the ground, bumped and stalled before coming to a stop a good ten meters from where Bob had come to rest.

Wally had seen the car, his car, hit the verge and disappear into the field, leaping from the Austin he ran to spot where his friend's body had been dumped.

He had never paid much attention to the First Aid demonstrations at work but, as a school boy, some of the rudimentary stuff they had been taught during the war must have stuck.

He knelt beside his friend,

"Bob, come on Bob, stop messing about." Wally had his head down, ear next to Bob's face, he couldn't hear any breathing.

Grabbing Bob's arm, Wally felt the wrist for a pulse.

He couldn't feel anything and gave up, cursing himself for wasting time.

He listened on Bob's chest, trying to be as still as he could so as not to miss the familiar beat which would tell him that Bob's heart was still alive. Nothing.

Irving could see Wally kneeling over Bob in the distance, the Leecher was over him like a wraith, reaching towards Wally's neck, drawing energy, getting stronger.

Irving screeched a war cry, determined to destroy the monstrosity before it destroyed him, the Leecher moved away from Wally, away from Bob and away from Irving.

Irving had never seen a Leecher in real-life, it was jagged and pulsed, unable to contain the raw energy it had sapped from its victims, sullying its haze with a dirty purple hue, seeing it in action filled Irving with repulsion and anger. By the time Irving reached Bob and Wally, the Leecher had gone, fleeing over the fields.

Irving had given chase, but only to make sure he would not be ambushed, before returning to the kneeling man who, by then, was crying over his friends' lifeless body.

Wally had tried pushing on Bob's chest and breathing into his mouth, Bob hadn't responded.

He sat for a moment, beaten and sobbing, before wiping his eyes and nose across his sleeve as he made his way back to the Austin to get a blanket from the boot.

Irving looked at the familiar body that lay in front of him, the orange marks on the neck still visible in the subdued sunlight, he had been too late this time.

He wondered if he should get to the nearest hospital and divine as soon as he could, or return to the council and tell them what he'd seen.

Better still he would hunt down the Leecher with his last drop of energy until he had either destroyed it or faded trying.

Wally had returned with the blanket, still sucking the snot and tears in short sobs, he gently unfurled the blanket and let it drift over Bob's prone body like a shroud.

He adjusted it slightly, tucking the edges under Bob's shoulders and knees, the blanket wasn't big enough to cover the whole of Bob at the same time, so Wally made sure the head was completely covered and left Bob's shoes peeking out from the edge of the blanket.

Before returning to the Austin, Wally removed the keys from the Triumph's ignition.

He started the five-mile journey to the next village where he would need to enlist the help of the local policeman to help him get Bob's body back home, then explain to Bob's parents what had happened to their son.

The noise of the Austin faded into the birdsong and windblown hedgerows, as Irving looked down on the covered body he wondered whether, had he arrived earlier and stopped the Leecher from drawing from Bob, Bob might have survived the impact.

There was no blood, no sign that Bob's body had received enough trauma, from hitting the tree, to kill him.

He could have stopped it.

He should have kept Bob alive and stopped the Leecher from taking all his energy.

Irving hated himself for not stopping the Leecher; hated the Leecher for killing Bob.

If he had hold of the Leecher, right now, Irving would make it put all the energy back, he would make it give it all back until it was empty, and Bob was alive.

But he didn't have hold of the Leecher, it was just Irving and Bob in a field, none of Bob's stolen life force and no way to give it back to Bob.

It planted the seed of an idea, it would be all or nothing.

He moved over Bob and reached into his chest.

Focusing all the energy within himself he began to concentrate, ball and gather all the energy that he had stored in preparation for his eventual divination.

The energy roared and rolled as Irving drew it together holding it inside as it grew, the strength trying to tear Irving in two, creating a second Watcher.

It grew and grew until Irving felt it rip at him, eager to break free, clawing for release.

He was ready to divine.

Irving focused on holding back the tidal wave of energy and then, just before the energy tore free, channelled it all into Bob's chest, flooding his heart with a surge of electricity.

Bob's body convulsed and stiffened as muscles reacted to the sudden jolt of energy.

His heart pushed blood into the vessels and organs, which had all but given up on oxygen, his brain sparked and told his lungs to stop buggering about and start breathing.

The rest of his organs received similar instructions and began clawing back into action, trying to catch-up on the shortfall caused by their brief demise.

Irving moved back in surprise.

Bob sat up.

Someone had covered him over with a blanket.

He pulled the blanket away from his face, blinked the dryness out of eyes and looked around.

He stopped and stared for a few moments,

"He's looking right at me." Irving thought.

It seemed that Bob was looking at him, not through him into the middle distance but directly at him.

Bob looked down, and moved the blanket off his legs, the rain had started to fall, lightly and in small flecks of water.

He got to his feet, cleared his throat and walked over to the triumph.

Noticing that the keys were no longer in the ignition, Bob set about the task of putting the roof up against the rain.

Five minutes later, and with the blanket folded neatly over his arm, Bob set off along the road in the direction of the nearest village.

Wally had confessed at the police station, he had told the sergeant how his friend was dead, how he'd probably been going too fast and about how he had planned to swap cars with Bob and drive the Triumph, uninsured, back to his house.

They had set off with the sergeant driving, a constable in the backseat and Wally in the passenger seat giving directions, heading back to where Wally had covered over his dead friend with a picnic blanket.

Three miles out of the village Wally shrieked and pointed at an oncoming pedestrian, who was carrying a folded blanket over his arm.

He grabbed at the steering wheel causing the police car to fishtail across the road.

"It's a ghost, he's come to haunt me!" Wally screamed at the sergeant before passing out in a faint.

An hour later it had all been sorted out back at the police station.

Wally had been convinced that Bob was not a ghost but had in fact been knocked unconscious by the tree and that, after Wally left, he had woken up and went in search of his friend.

The constable had driven the Triumph back to the station where Wally could pick it up the next day so long as he took his driver's licence and proof of insurance with him.

The constable then drove both men home in the Austin with Bob receiving advice to go to the hospital and get himself checked up, just in case the knock on the head had shaken anything loose.

So, in the early evening, after a brief 'all clear' at the Doctors Surgery, Bob lay on his bed next to an exhausted, drained Irving and went to sleep.

A question of faith

Bob sat in the congregation, not singing the hymns or bowing his head in prayer but listening intently to the sermon which the Reverend had been delivering in the cold, stone church for the last half an hour, against the soft murmuring of the rain from outside.

The sermon had been about the nature of true sacrifice, using the story of Abraham as a reference.

Father Molyneux had explained that sacrifice should not be a burden or done in a half-hearted manor, as true sacrifice was its own reward.

Bob made a mental note to point out that, if he took anyone up a mountain and tried to sacrifice them he'd be locked up in an asylum and probably not revered as a prophet.

But right now, he had more important questions which needed answering.

"It was nice to see you in the congregation this morning Robert," Father Molyneux stood at the door of the church and addressed each member of the congregation as they filed out into the rain-soaked morning, "will we be seeing you on a regular basis?"

"Probably not Vicar," Bob answered honestly, "I have a question which I though you would be the best person to answer."

"Oh, right, well this sounds interesting." The Vicar rubbed his hands together in anticipation, "let me finish up here and I'll try to answer your questions, over a cup of tea in the vicarage maybe."

Bob agreed and went to get his bike, which he wheeled to the vicarage, while Father Molyneux spoke to each of the dwindling assembly until he was left alone to lock the church door.

He then joined Bob at the vicarage.

The kettle was placed onto the hob plate of the wood stove and left to boil, as Father Molyneux spooned loose tea into a silver strainer.

He got two cups and matching saucers from the sideboard and placed them in readiness, the strainer was then lowered into the simmering kettle.

Bob confirmed that he did indeed take milk but declined the offer of sugar lumps.

Father Molyneux carried both cups in and, placing one cup in front of Bob and the other opposite, returned to the kitchen briefly for the biscuit tin.

"Right Robert, let's see if we can't provide an answer to your questions, shall we?" The Vicar had subjected the biscuit, held between finger and thumb, to a thorough dunking into the cup of milky tea.

Bob had given this question some considerable thought in the days that had passed since the accident.

He looked at the Vicar, looked at the tea drenched biscuit and decided to ask the question as was, without beating around any bushes.

"What does the Devil look like?"

Father Molyneux chewed and swallowed, clearing his palate of biscuity bits,

"Well Robert, the Devil takes on many forms, gluttony, sloth, avarice to name but a few." Bob interrupted.

"No Vicar, I mean what does he look like, his physical appearance. Does the Bible describe the Devil's physical appearance anywhere?" The Vicar thought for a moment.

"Yes, I believe it does." Father Molyneux got to his feet and walked over to a stout bookshelf that stood against the wall at the far end of the room.

Skimming over the spines of bound theological tomes his finger hovered over a large King James Bible, which he then drew out of the ranks and returned with it to where Bob was seated.

Bob perched forward on the seat in anticipation,

"Well Vicar?"

Vicar Molyneux found the passage and cleared his throat,

"Thou hast been in Eden the garden of God; every precious stone thy covering, the Sardius, topaz, and the diamond, the beryl, the onyx, and the jasper, the sapphire, the emerald, and the carbuncle, and gold: the workmanship of thy tabrets and of thy pipes was prepared in thee in the day that thou wast created."

He lowered the book and looked across at Bob. "Lucifer was the barer of light before he was cast down, he was the highest of the Angels, there is a description of the cherubim if you're interested?" Bob nodded, as the Vicar flicked through a few pages and continued reading.

"And their whole body, and their backs, and their hands, and their wings, and the wheels, were full of eyes round about, even the wheels that they four had. As for the wheels, it was cried unto them in my hearing, O wheel. And every one had four faces: the first face was the face of a cherub, and the second face was the face of a man, and the third the face of a lion, and the fourth the face of an eagle."

The book was closed carefully before the Vicar put it to one side and picked up his tea cup.

Bob was thinking about the descriptions, he half raised his cup of tea then paused.

"He's not just a shadow? the Devil I mean; he doesn't just look like a kind of shadow but in the air?"

"Not according to Ezekiel, I imagine Lucifer would look very much like an Angel, splendid and awe inspiring with wings covered in eyes, wheels and four different faces. Why the sudden interest Robert?" The Vicar looked concerned.

"I'm not sure Vicar, when I came to, after the accident, I could swear I saw something, I thought maybe it was the Devil or the grim reaper and I thought if anyone would know, it would be you." Bob sipped at his tea.

In the kitchen, Irving was arguing with More towels, "If the council want to see me so badly they can come and see ME!" Irving was adamant that, from now on, Bob would receive his full attention.

"That's not how it works Irving, the council need you to explain what the Hell it is that you've been doing; and you can't expect all of them to come traipsing around after you all over the countryside."

"Well if they want any answers from me, that's what they are going to have to do because I'm not letting Bob out of my sight for one more second from now on, Okay?"

"They think you're the Leecher Irving, and who can blame them? You leave meetings, you refuse to attend meetings, if I didn't know you better I think I'd probably believe you were the Leecher."

"I saw it More towels, it nearly killed Bob, I can't protect him if I'm caught up in another meeting with a council that doesn't seem to want to do anything about anything, until every Watcher has faded."

Irving wasn't going to attend another council meeting and More towels knew it, he wasn't sure how he would relay the conversation to the council along with Irving's refusal to attend any further meetings.

"They're not going to be happy Irving; they expect an explanation."

In the sitting room the conversation continued,

"An accident like that must have been very traumatic Robert, I'm not surprised that your thoughts would be focused on the religious aspect of your mortality; it doesn't mean that the grim reaper is stalking you."

Bob felt some of the tension, which had balled up inside him since the accident, ease a little.

The Vicar continued,

"You may have imagined the presence of this apparition or what you might have visualized was some sort of guardian angel, sent to protect you."

He paused to swirl, then sip at the tea in the bottom of the cup,

"In any case Robert, real or imagined, it makes no difference, so long as you choose to believe, what you saw will remain real to you."

Bob nodded his head, thinking about the Vicars', offered, perspective.

In the kitchen, Irving was still refusing to meet the council on any of More towel's terms.

"As a young boy, I used to make up imaginary friends Robert," the priest had bridged his fingers in a steeple and was gazing into the distance, "as an only child I had no one else to play with so I invented friends. By my mother's accounts, the games I would play were somewhat convoluted and occasionally ended in arguments, between myself and my imaginary friends."

The Vicar focused on Bob once more. "The point I'm trying to make, Robert, is that the friends, although imaginary to everyone else, were real to me. I can look back on a childhood without any loneliness and I'm convinced, more than ever, that the Lord had a hand in making sure I was not without friends." The empty tea cup clinked onto the saucer as the vicar placed it to one side.

"What you believe you saw is the only thing that is important Robert, to my mind the fact that we are here enjoying a cup of tea can only suggest that the thing you saw was not evil and not pursuant of your demise."

"But it couldn't have been my guardian angel because it didn't have wheels." Replied Bob, jokily.

"Right you are Robert." Father Molyneux laughed, took the empty tea cup from Bob and returned them to the kitchen.

"So, I can tell the council that you will meet with them but only if they come to you, that you can explain your whereabouts during your absences from the previous meetings and that you can give them a description of the Leecher now?" More towels had summed up the heated debate in a sentence, Irving ran through the list quickly.

"Yep, that about covers it." He replied, watching Bob standing and shaking Father Molyneux's hand then waiting for the Vicar to return with his coat.

"They won't like it Irving." More towels called after Irving as Bob and the Watcher left the cozy vicarage and stepped into the light but constant rain.

Bob peddled his bike slowly, not concerned by the beads of water which melted into his clothes, his mind was on the things which Father Molyneux had said, Irving stayed beside him, vigilantly watching for the slightest sign of danger.

The rain continued through the night and into the morning, the grey clouds filling the sky with hopelessness and disappointment.

Bob pedaled his bike around the larger puddles, the waterproof poncho keeping him dry whilst giving the impression that he had been underneath a huge disc of falling yellow pastry.

Irving stayed close by, ready to act on the slightest tingle, although Bob was feeling his normal self, Irving knew that he was not back to full strength.

He hadn't drawn from Bob since the accident and, as a result, was dangerously low on energy himself.

The Leecher had got to him, nearly faded him by killing Bob, Irving wasn't sure how he had managed to save Bob.

As weak as he was, Irving had decided to fight and he wasn't about to let the council stand in his way.

He had to admit that More towels was right, he did look guilty, he had ducked out of two meetings and had no alibi for the last two Leecher attacks.

Now the council would ask for him again but this time he would not go, he figured he would probably be sanctioned at very least.

The worst the council could do would be to cast him out, he would be marked and thrown out of the community.

Leaving Bob on his own and turning Irving into a wandering specter, destined to fade or leech like a monstrous parasite, gorging on life force like an addict.

Bob's day at work was uneventful, Wally kept looking at him nervously, almost as if he was waiting for Bob to vanish in to thin air, leaving a pile of clothes.

Wally had even poked him on the shoulder at lunch time,

"You were dead Bob, I swear it." He had offered in explanation when Bob had shot him a stern look and thumped him on the shoulder,

"Well, how's that for dead?" Bob chuckled in reply.

Irving was glad when the end of the working day was punctuated by the claxon.

The ride home was slow going, the rain had increased, both in volume and force, and showed no sign of tiring.

Approaching the farm house through the haze of rain, Irving could see the shape of More towels waiting for him by the door, Bob parked his bike in the barn next to a straw bale, and went into the house.

"Hello More towels, not a social visit I guess." Irving moved into the hall way, leaving More towels to trail in after him.

From the kitchen, Bob's mother called through to Bob,

"Bobby keep your coat on, Lucy's out again, go fetch her and get her back in her coop before I throttle the little so and so."

Bob dripped through the front room and out into the back yard.

The bright yellow poncho acted as a beacon for the small bantam who was not mesmerized, due to Irving's absence and was hell bent on resisting capture.

Inside the farm house More towels was trying a new tack.

"Irving, regardless of what the council think of you, you're the only Watcher who has seen the Leecher and survived, you need to tell them what you saw so we can catch it and destroy it." Irving sensed that More towels had not told the council of his refusal to attend any further meetings.

"I told you before," Irving was standing strong this time, determined to stick to his guns, "if the council wants to see me they can come to me, I'm not leaving Bob unguarded, not after what happened last time."

"They need to know Irving; you have to tell them." More towels was almost begging, "I can watch Bob if you're worried about leaving him on his own, I can watch him while you go to the council, straight there straight back, no more than half an hour, I won't let Bob out of my sight I promise."

"Thanks for the offer More towels, but as I said before, the council can come to me, I'm not going to be miles away the next time Bob is in danger, and I'm not going to have you on my conscience if the Leecher tries to get to Bob again." Irving was resolute.

Although he was still very weak having not replenished his energy since the accident, he was not about to expose his exhaustion to anyone.

He imagined a puffed-up Bullfrog arched up on all fours, Irving hoped the façade was convincing.

Next week Bob would be able to support Irving's nightly draw, until then Irving would have to get by on smoke and mirrors.

More towels seemed frustrated with Irving's steadfast stubbornness but finally resigned himself to Irving's final answer.

"I'll tell the council, Irving for your sake I hope you know what you're doing." The meeting was over.

In the backyard the chase continued, soggy chicken versus The Yellow Poncho monster, the chicken was in the lead.

As More towels reached the wall Irving called out to him,

"Where's father Molyneux?" Irving had just realized that, unusually, More towels had come alone.

More towels paused at the wall,

"What are you insinuating…" He stopped himself from finishing the sentence, "He's at a church meeting Irving, he's being watched so I can come out to try and talk some sense into you. Maybe you should give a little thought to your own position rather than worrying about mine." More towels turned away a left through the wall.

Irving stood for a moment, turning the conversation over in his mind before heading out into the backyard to assist a giant, flapping, yellow traffic cone to incarcerate the bantam that had been proving so allusive.

Under suspicion

It was Saturday morning and Bob had woken with stomach ache. It wasn't debilitating, it wasn't even that painful, it was more of an annoyance and it had put him off his breakfast.

He was helping his dad on the top field for most of the morning.

The corn stubble, which stood out of the ground like a day-old beard, had to be ploughed back into the soil before the field would be ready for planting potatoes.

Bob was up on the tractor watching the plough bite into the dirt and fold the rich dark earth over on itself, it hadn't been that long ago that he and his Dad would have hitched up a team of horses and walked the field.

The tractor was relentless, as a Dakota flew low over the field and briefly drowned out the diesel engine with the throb and hum of twin propellers, Bob's growling stomach reminded him that he had foregone his breakfast.

He retrieved an apple from his jacket pocket and bit into the side, hoping to satisfy his stomach for a few more hours; his appetite had still not returned.

He could still hear the dull drum of the airplane as it landed at the airfield a few miles away, it's engines slowing then revving as it taxied towards a hanger, during the war he had watched the fighter planes roar up into the sky in waves, to do battle amongst the birds and clouds.

Now the horses were gone and the fighters were gone, leaving Bob gently swaying and rocking on top of the undulating tractor.

Watching the neat rows appear out of the soil, he wondered why the apple had all the appeal of a raw parsnip.

The tractor crept up and down the field for most of the morning until the straggly corn stubs had been combed into neat rows of tilled earth.

Bob settled the tractor at the edge of the field and switched off the grumbling engine which rattled then fell silent.

"All this technology is bloody noisy." He thought to himself, thumbing open the grease proof paper which encased his sandwiches; sandwiches which were considered for a second before being rewrapped and replaced into the box next to the tractor seat, he would eat them later.

Bob drew out the shotgun, with which he intended to spend his afternoon.

He had finally decided to replace the one that, after his run in with the combine harvester, was no longer straight.

He had bought it from Virginia Orton as she gradually went through Henry's effects, that she would never use, and sold them on to local farmers.

It wasn't a bad gun, sturdy and a little lighter than the Russian artillery piece which used to be his hunting companion.

Bob checked the barrels before swinging it over his shoulder, stepping from the tractor and heading towards the hedge line.

He sat on a slight rise of grass at the foot of the hedgerow, hefted the gun off his shoulder and thumbed two cartridges into the hollow barrels.

He laid back against the lump of grass allowing the cacophony of nature to close over him.

The clouds rushed over birds which swooped and flitted urgently amongst the eddies, unconcerned by the reclining, solitary audience below.

Crows, like ink blots, landed amongst the ridges of turned mud to peck at the worms and grubs which had been unceremoniously unearthed.

The ebony throng were soon noticed, and joined, by wood pigeons whose numbers grew until the field had a mottled grey coating which bobbed along the earthen isles.

Bob had closed his eyes and was in the space between sleep and consciousness, his mind slipping its lead to throw all manner of imaginations into the mixture of thoughts and dreams.

In his mind, Bob could run fast, leaping over trees and houses, almost flying.

He ran across the countryside in bounds, not tiring, not faltering.

Soon he could see the sea, speeding up he reached the cliff edge and gave an almighty jump, springing into the air, leaving the ground beneath him.

Over the water, the cliffs looked tiny as he passed through clouds, he wondered how he would land, the thought took over like poison, would it hurt?

His stomach started to turn, maybe he'd jumped too high, the graceful leap became an elongated fall, Bob no longer able to control his decent, tumbling through the air.

The birds cooed around him, then Bob was awake, the pigeons had pulled him out of his trance.

He allowed the tumbling in his stomach to settle.

Shouldering the shotgun, he peppered three birds who were close enough to each other for both barrels to encompass them all.

In the distance, Irving could see the approaching Watchers, as they grew closer it became apparent that the council had come to him.

The assembled Watchers formed a semicircle around Irving as Bob collected the dead pigeons, reloaded the gun and settled back to wait for the other pigeons, who would soon forget about the loud noise and subsequent loss of their comrades.

Irving answered the questions; the meeting was more to the point this time.

The questions were direct and, in their nature, confirmed More towels suggestion that Irving was now firmly under suspicion.

He had explained the situations leading up to this point in time.

He told them about the Leecher, about his decision to leave the two previous meetings along with his decision not to attend any more council meetings.

Irving told them everything, except for how he had used his divining energy to bring Bob back to life.

The congregated Watchers seemed content that Irving had given them the whole story, Are you alright Mortimer assured Irving that the council "Would be in touch."

As an exclamation mark at the end of the meeting, My goodness me Grace added, "I'm watching you Irving."

Then they left, Irving watched them disappear into the distance before returning to stand sentinel over the field.

The council had imposed a curfew on Irving.

His reluctance to attend the council's investigation a reason to insist Irving should never be far enough away to lose sight of Bob.

The curfew seemed to be in Irving's favour but, with the warning of consequences should Irving be seen out on his own, would be taken seriously.

Bob had bagged another five pigeons, which now lay in a cloth sack behind the driver's seat of the open top tractor that Bob was jockeying home.

His stomach had started aching again, slightly more persistently than the dull ache which had presented itself over the last twenty-four hours.

His appetite was still absent and, all in all, Bob thought he must be coming down with a stomach bug or some sort of exotic virus.

Some milk of magnesia and an aspirin when he got home would soon have him feeling better.

That night Bob was restless, the milk of magnesia sat in his stomach like chalky bile and threatened to rout its meagre contents which remained undigested.

The ache in his guts had grown steadily throughout the day and was, for the first time, painful rather than just annoying.

Irving followed Bob down stairs and waited in the kitchen while Bob filled the kettle and placed it on the stove, removing the whistle so as not to wake his Mum or Dad.

He and Irving sat, eventually watching the sunrise announce its impeding arrival by staining the sky with an orange hue.

Bob was tired, his stomach ache was persisting, the cup of tea not denting the pain.

For the first-time Irving was aware of the slight tingle which had settled on him, it was faint and distant and hadn't grown in the same way that usually portended Bob's downfall.

Irving was jumpy, he checked the house and surrounding horizon, the light tingle made him uneasy.

There was no vision not even the briefest flash, he stared into the morning, wondering if the Leecher was watching him unseen.

He was still very weak, and he knew he would need to draw soon.

Bob washed himself and prepared for work.

The morning mist was settling in pockets, wherever the ground undulated little pools of thick air gathered and hung, the brightening sky proof of the Sun's threat to burst over the horizon.

He took a pan full of grain into the yard and, after opening the chicken coop, scattered the little wheat pips in great sweeps, much to the delight of the sleepy hens.

He watched as the chaotic pecking became a synchronised pattern of bobbing brown heads, picking off the grains one by one.

Bob's mum had talked about getting a cow to milk, and although Bob's father had dismissed the idea with initial concerns of lack of space.

Bob knew it wouldn't take long for his mum to tie his dad into a Gordian knot of reason.

Besides, she had already cleared a space in the yard as proof of her point.

Inside he warmed a slice of bread over the range, which he had restocked with wood, before replacing the refilled kettle over the softly popping fire.

The whistle reinstated on the spout, he smeared some marmalade over one corner of freshly crisped toast and bit into the syrupy zest, the tang refreshingly sharp.

Hopeful that his appetite had returned, Bob smeared marmalade over the remaining toast and set about finishing the slice of toast in large, sticky bites before noisily sucking each finger clean.

The whistle from the stove grew to a crescendo before Bob's mum moved it from the stove and prepared the tea pot for a fresh brew.

"You're up early Bobby, everything okay?" The question came from within the flurry of tealeaves, strainers and milk jugs.

"Couldn't sleep, had a funny tummy." Bob replied, swiping at a crumb which had stuck itself just under his nose.

"You feeling okay now?" She asked, "take some milk of magnesia, that should settle it."

The tea pot was placed on the side to brew, as the familiar bumping and grumbling from the ceiling meant that Bob's dad was pulling himself out of bed.

Irving watched as the household gradually gathered speed, until Bob's mum was preparing the laundry to be washed, Bob's dad was pulling his boots on in the hallway and Bob was wheeling his bike out of the shed and snaking it through the oblivious brood of pecking chickens in the yard.

The day had begun.

Irving intervened early, Bob had pulled the bolt across on the blind side of the gate and turned to walk his bike onto the road, the bolt had missed the catch allowing the gate to slowly swing open under its own weight.

Irving wondered if this was the cause of the tingle which had been bothering him recently.

He formed a small magnetic charge that pulled at the door key in Bob's pocket, flicking it out onto the stone path.

The metallic 'ping' drew Bob's eye to where the key had landed and, upon retrieving it, drew attention to the gradually opening gate.

Pocketing the key, Bob went back to fasten the bolt properly, ensuring the bolt had engaged properly this time.

He imagined the scene, coming home from work and having to chase the liberated chickens.

"That was lucky." Bob told himself, swinging himself onto the bike saddle and pedalling slowly to the printing works, Irving following closely.

The clumps of mist slowed the journey down forcing Bob to watch the road closely to miss pot holes.

On a couple of occasions he became a moving target for the cars, which swerved to avoid the lone cyclist as they sped through the close, damp air.

Irving watched, making sure Bob was out of the way before the cars got too close, steering him with little jolts of electricity directly to muscles like the reins of a cart horse.

He was still aware of the tingle; it hadn't grown in strength but hadn't diminished despite Irving's most recent interventions and, for that reason, was becoming a concern.

"Maybe the tingle has something to do with My goodness me Grace's promise or threat that he would be watching me."

The idea began to take root in Irving's imagination as he and Bob, gingerly, crossed the railway crossing which stood between the farm and the printing works.

It grew stronger as Irving tried to pick it apart; the tingle meant that Bob was in danger and if it was related to My goodness me Grace, then it meant My goodness me Grace was a danger to Bob.

"Was My goodness me Grace the Leecher?" Irving was horrified at the notion he had uncovered but it made perfect sense, "My goodness me Grace was from out of town, he could have leeched Greville and faded You bastard, could have drawn from Father Molyneux and the two infants."

The dots were quickly joining up for Irving until he hit the catch,

"My goodness me Grace was in the meeting which he left to save Bob's life from the Leecher." Irving struggled to rebuild the connection.

"Maybe My goodness me Grace was just helping the Leecher, an inside man so to speak." Regardless of My goodness me Grace's involvement with the Leecher, Irving was going to watch him like a hawk from now on.

The uncomfortable pain in Bob's abdomen had grown as the day progressed, making him wince and pull up once or twice.

His lunch remained un-eaten and stomach churned and grumbled its complaint.

The sun had burnt through the morning mist but, as the early afternoon faded, the clouds pulled across the sky and cast a stinging wind into the grey air.

Bob pedalled against the eddies which charged at him like a stubborn goat, trying to slow him to a standstill.

The prevailing gusts and the growling, aching stomach had made Bob irritable.

With a strong gust that knocked Bob to one side, forcing his foot onto the dirt to keep him vertical. Bob swore, as loud as he could at the grey clouds and pitiless wind currents.

A shout which the wind whipped away and tore into a muffled murmur, as it continued to buffet Bob and his bike.

The sense that Bob was in danger, probably from My goodness me Grace, was comforting for Irving.

It gave him a focus, a direction to watch for danger, although the tingle hadn't gained enough substance to offer Irving a glimpse into the near future.

The revelation, to Irving's mind, gave him the jump on the Leecher, the odious THING which had drained Bob once, to death, and had left him with the promise that he, Irving, was being watched. Irving could feel the anger and contempt building inside him, he had given it a face, My goodness me Grace's face.

At the first sign of danger or attack, Irving knew he would disappear My goodness me Grace.

Even if it meant expending all his energy, Irving was prepared to fade if it meant keeping Bob alive.

After all, Irving had divined once already and in Bob was half of Irving.

Bob, eventually, wheeled his bike into the farmyard and secured it in the shed.

The ride home had taken a lot out of him and after declining him mother's offer of a cup of tea, shook his shoes off in the hall before making his way up the stairs and getting into bed.

Irving watched Bob pull the covers over his head and listened to the breathing slow into a deeper rhythm before stationing himself at the foot of Bob's bed.

He settled back and let his mind wander over recent events, trying to make sense of the situation he found himself in the middle of.

Bob had been in bed asleep for just over an hour, Irving resting at the foot of the bed like the hound at his master's feet on an old stone effigy, before a stark brief image and sense of acute agony brought Irving up with a start.

He looked for the danger, for the Leecher, for My goodness me Grace.

There was no one else and nothing else in the room.

Irving checked the hallway, then the other rooms in the farm house, returning to Bob quickly to reassure himself that everything was still okay.

The image hadn't shown Irving very much, just Bob lying still, his face contorted with pain.

No wounds and no reason for Bob's imminent departure, but the sense of pain was real.

Irving knew Bob's life was, once again, right on the edge.

He kept watch into the night, wishing he was stronger, wondering if he could safely draw from Bob but knowing he couldn't leave him that weak, no matter what.

He would just have to fight smart and hope that he could get enough of a jump, on the Leecher, to make a difference.

The clock on the mantelpiece suggested that the day was just about three hours old when Bob was woken by a sharp dig in his gut.

It caused him to wince and curl up like a woodlouse, his knees tucked close into his chest.

The pain subsided but left the underlying ache that had ground Bob down over the past few days.

Gradually he unfurled and eased himself out of bed.

Donning a well-worn dressing gown Bob made his way downstairs to the bathroom where, after opening the medicine cabinet, he located the aspirin and an opened bottle of milk of magnesia, the former being swallowed with help from a mouthful of the latter.

After a moment for consideration, he lifted the toilet seat and began the formalities to empty his bladder.

Bob had read about exotic fish which, under the right circumstances, would swim up the urethra of anyone ignorant enough to urinate into their patch of river.

Once in the urethra their dorsal spines would discourage and prevent extraction.

Bob wondered if the sensation of having a tiny, spiny, fish in your willy was the same as the sensation which currently plagued his guts.

He imagined that the only way to extract the fish would be to kill it, by hitting the relevant area with a wooden mallet before extracting the dead fish.

He made a mental note never to pee into any river, foreign or domestic.

For the next hour and a half Bob sat in an arm chair, his knees raised under his chin, the pain was enough to keep sleep at bay but not enough to send him running to the doctors.

He had already run through a list, in his head, of everything he'd eaten recently.

He was satisfied that shellfish, or fish of any kind, had not been part of his diet since the last time he had visited the seaside, four or five months ago.

Irving was aware that the danger, of which the tingle was a symptom, was not immediate but he needed to know more.

"Catch the tingle early." He could hear his own advice.

He could remember when it was passed on to him, he had caught the tingle early now if he only knew what to do with it.

The rain began hard.

It hit the roof tiles and windows with the eagerness of a door to door salesman.

Testing the house for cracks or holes through which it could seep into, to get at the woodwork and plaster and make everything damp.

The noise grew as the size of the raindrops and their frequency increased, it sounded like the hiss of static on the wireless and made Bob cover his ears against its persistent force.

Bob was laying on the ground next to the printing machine.

The image flashed before Irving, it was brief but unmistakable, Bob would die at work unless Irving did something about it.

He still didn't know the cause or manner of the threat, but it was a start, something for Irving to go on.

He thought about Bob's work place, so many things could happen.

Bob hadn't been crushed or impaled, Irving was certain, there was no blood.

That didn't rule out electrocution, heart failure, poisoning, brain haemorrhage, snake bite, the list went on and on.

Irving was stuck,

"How can I watch for all those things?" He asked himself, although he already knew the answer, he couldn't.

Irving tried to look at the situation from every angle, it usually helped him come up with a solution.

His information was patchy at best and left too many things to chance, too many things to guard against.

There was no way he could protect Bob at his work place, the answer unfurled in front of him.

Irving didn't need to keep Bob safe, he just needed to keep Bob away from the printing works and that was simple.

Bob was still curled up on the armchair when Irving started to draw.

A wave of nausea followed by fatigue and lethargy, crawled over Bob.

It ran down his neck and made his legs and arms numb.

His head felt heavy and lolled forward, his neck no longer able or willing to prop up the weight against gravity.

Bob felt dizzy, his eyes blinked closed and then he was asleep.

Irving hoped he hadn't drawn too much, Bob's now resting figure was still weak, but Irving had been careful, now he would have to wait and watch.

"Bobby?"

Bob opened his eyes; the rain was still heavy outside but the static hiss had turned into a clatter and splosh as the puddles deepened.

"Are you okay Bobby?" His mum was standing over him, looking concerned.

"What time is it?" Bob asked, aware that it was a work day and he was going to get wet, by the looks of things, very wet.

"It's quarter to eight." This sent a jolt through Bob, he was going to be late for work, he uncurled and started to stand until a sharp pang through his stomach sat him back down.

"I've phoned your work and told 'em you're not coming in today," his mum was frowning at him, more through concern rather than disapproval, "and I've called for the district nurse, so you just stay sat there till she gets here."

Bob knew that this wasn't an order, nor was it a request, it was the way things were going to be.

He sat back in the chair.

Twenty minutes later a yellow speck in the distance grew into a poncho weaving along the road through rain dented puddles.

Gradually the poncho grew large enough to push the bike onto its stand under the eaves of one of the tractor sheds.

It retrieved a medical bag from the wicker basket, which was attached to the handlebars, and stepped through the doorway which Bob's mum was holding open.

Bob listened to the rustle of wet poncho and small talk coming from the hall way, as the poncho shed her yellow chrysalis and emerged through the door as nurse Linda.

"Right Robert," the announcement was on the fierce side of sturdy and Bob was slightly taken aback, "you do realise that you don't have to keep injuring yourself as an excuse to see more of me, you could just ask me to go to the pictures with you."

Bob was flustered, the way his mum was laughing meant that he had gone red.

Linda was smiling as he floundered for a few seconds before she took the reins once again.

"So, what's the matter?" She looked up from the medical bag briefly, before continuing with her search. "Ahha." She held the thermometer aloft.

"I'm feeling a bit tired," Bob offered, "haven't been sleeping too well for the last couple of nights."

The thermometer was wiped in alcohol, dried, then placed under Bob's tongue.

"Any pain, fever, vomiting?" The nurse was staring intently at her pocket watch, as if timing Bob's reply.

"Um, yeah, a lithle bith of a thtomach ache." Bob responded, the thin glass straw rattling against his teeth.

"Right," Linda removed the thermometer and looked at the measure of mercury, "Opps, wrong thermometer, this is the rectal one."

She smiled as she shook the mercury back down and wiped it over with alcohol before it went back into its case and into the medical bag.

"Just kidding, and your temperature is normal." Bob was slightly relieved but still feeling quite nervous.

"You've had stomach ache, how long for?" Bob thought for a few moments,

"He hasn't been right since Friday or Saturday." His mum had offered the answer to speed things along.

"How's your appetite been Robert?" Linda looked more serious now, the joking had left her voice.

"Not great..." Bob started,

"He's probably only had a bit of toast in the last few days, isn't that right Bobby?" His mum chipped in again.

"Okay, let's give this a try. Can you lay on the sofa on your back for me Robert?"

Bob walked slowly over to the sofa and unfurled, mindful of any stabs of pain as he finally lay flat, looking up at the ceiling.

"Can you lift your vest up for me." The nurse was standing over Bob looking at his stomach.

"Is that enough?" Bob had rolled his vest up to the bottom of his ribcage and was waiting for the next set of orders.

"Yes, that's fine, now this might be a little uncomfortable."

Linda had placed two fingers onto the right side of Bob's abdomen, just above the top of his hip, "Does that hurt at all?" She pushed her fingers into Bob's side, making a dimple in the side of his stomach.

"A little bit, it's not too bad."

"How about when I let go?"

The nurse swiftly removed the pressure from Bob's gut and unleashed a spasm of agony, which leapt around Bob's body, curling him up with a yell of pain.

"Yep, that will be your appendix then."

"But I haven't finished yet." Bob joked through the tears, which had gathered near his nose, in response to the dagger that he could still feel where the nurse's fingers had been.

"You can pull your vest down now Robert." Linda walked over to where Bob's mum had been watching the performance.

"May I borrow your phone?" She asked, "I'm going to call for an Ambulance." Bob's mum looked horrified.

"Why does he need an Ambulance?" The sudden worry evident in her voice.

"Just a precaution, his appendix is quite swollen, an ambulance will be able to get him to the hospital faster than I could on my bike."

Bob's mum showed the nurse to the small cupboard, under the stairs.

The phone sat on a small writing desk near a small, chewed pencil and a note book with scribbled jots of numbers and scraps of relevant information and redundant potato prices.

Bob could hear the dial wound clockwise before being released to spin anticlockwise in a smooth, mechanical hum.

Linda spoke to the operator on the other end, confirming his details and the nature of the emergency in a very professional manner before reappearing at the door.

"The Ambulance is on its way, do you want to get a few things together, toothbrush, slippers, dressing gown, that sort of thing. I'm afraid you're going to have a couple of nights in the hospital Robert."

Bob's mum now had something to focus her energy, she whirled into action, organising an overnight bag for Bob.

"How long will I need to be in hospital?"

Bob wasn't keen on hospitals.

He had never liked visiting people who were sick, it's seemed a little voyeuristic.

He liked the idea of having to stay in hospital even less.

"Hopefully only a few days, your appendix is quite inflamed, but they should be able to whip it out before it bursts, if it does, you might need to stay a little while longer."

"Oh, okay." Bob hoped it wouldn't burst.

Five minutes later a flash of blue and the distant Banshee wail announced the impending Ambulance.

Bob's mum was ready, she had packed a small suitcase which included Bob's pyjamas, toothbrush, half a tube of Crest toothpaste, one weeks change of underpants, three vests, two pairs of trousers, five shirts, five pairs of socks and a packet of Maynard's wine gums.

She had also stowed two books on top of the white Y-fronts, one by Enid Blyton the other by Ian Fleming, in case Bob got bored of lying in bed staring at the ceiling.

The Ambulance arrived in the front yard, crunching the wet gravel and muddy puddles, the blue lights lingering in the raindrops that ran down the window pane.

Bob could hear a door open then shut, then a second.

The deeper squeak, of the rear double doors, was shortly followed by the crunch of footsteps and the light rattle of a sturdy wheelchair.

The front door was opened by Linda who ushered the driver and porter towards their cargo.

The two men, after giving a cheery "Good morning" to both Linda and Bob's mum, then set about lifting Bob off the sofa and into the chair.

One man swung Bob's legs around to get him into a sitting position then, each man under an armpit, they stood Bob up and expertly deposited him into the leather seat of the wheelchair.

One man then took up position behind the chair while the other took control of Bob's suit case, before making their way back out into the rain towards the Ambulance.

They lifted Bob, chair and all, into the back.

The porter followed Bob and shut the doors from the inside, while the driver went back round to the cab and brought the engine back to life.

Bob had dissuaded his mum from coming along to the hospital with him,

"I won't be long mum, probably just a few hours and I'll be out again. Besides you'll just be sitting around waiting for most of the time, honestly I'll be fine."

His mum finally capitulated and told Bob that she and his father would come to the hospital once he had finished in the fields for the day.

The Ambulance trundled through the ruts and dips of the farm yard before reaching the road, picking up speed and turning the siren back on.

Bob's mum watched it into the distance before shutting the door and heading back into the living room.

Linda had almost re-packed her medical back, folding an eye bandage back into a neat square and placing it back over the cylindrical thermometer case.

"Would you like a cup of tea?" Bob's mum asked, "it doesn't look like the rain is easing up at all." The medical bag was finally closed and fastened shut.

"Yes, that might be nice." Linda replied, following Bob's mum into the kitchen to help brew the tea and, at the same time, put her mind at ease that Bob would be okay.

In the ambulance, Irving watched the porter checking Bob's blood pressure, record the reading onto the chart which was pinched, tightly, to a clipboard.

They raced through the countryside every jolt sending a spasm of pain through Bob's abdomen.

The porter, unfazed by the rocking and lurching, began asking Bob a series of questions about the pain.

What and when he had last eaten, any allergies, injuries as well as recent occurrences which may have contributed to Bob's present condition.

Although Irving was having to concentrate quite hard to keep pace with the ambulance, to keep up with Bob, he was also aware that the tingle had become a shiver.

Now more than ever, he needed to stay alert.

They would soon be in the lion's den of danger and disease.

The ambulance slowed as it approached the hospital, turning onto the narrow, inner road which wove around the hospital grounds, finally coming to a halt outside of Accident and Emergency.

The rear doors were opened, and ramps extended out to the floor.

Bob was wheeled back down onto the tarmac, then hurried into the reception area.

His present condition fast tracked Bob through the normal process and made him a priority.

He was checked and rechecked by doctors and consultant's, before the appearance of a surgeon in Bob's cubicle signalled bad news for Bob's appendix.

"We need to operate immediately... Robert." The surgeon mumbled as a matter of fact, reading the notes which hung from the foot of the gurney Bob was currently lying upon. "Frankly I'll be surprised if your appendix hasn't exploded already, we'll have to hose your guts out before we stitch you back up, it's fantastically messy and a right ruddy pain in the arse. SOMEBODY PREP THIS APPENDIX AND GET HIM DOWN TO THEATRE!"

With that he turned and left, like a ham actor, the curtain wafting closed behind him.

And that was it, Bob was about to have his appendix removed, he could feel the nerves in his stomach, the apprehension made his throat tight and hot.

But he was in the system now, the mechanisms began to whirl.

Bob was moved, on the gurney, out of the cubicle into the corridor, along the corridor passed the wide stairs to the wide doors.

A sign on the doors designating them as a 'Staff lift only' the instructions in smaller writing underneath instructed 'Gurneys to the right.'

Irving felt as apprehensive as Bob, the shiver was very strong now the danger was all around.

Irving was watching for stray needles, murderous electrodes and anyone who looked like they may have contracted a contagious lurgy.

All that on top of the knowledge that the real threat, the Leecher, might be waiting around every corner.

A few floors down and Bob was wheeled out of the lift towards 'Pre-Op'.

Into a small room where a team of four people, already masked and gowned, administered various concoctions into the vein on the back of Bob's right hand.

It made him drowsy and a nauseating dizziness began to muddle his thoughts, almost as if his brain was slowly being filled with thick, viscous glue.

A mask was placed over his nose and mouth and a hollow, far away voice told him to count to ten.

"One... Two... Three... ... ... Four,"

Bob was aware of a shadow in the corner of the room, the same shadow he had seen after the car accident, "whaass..."

And he was asleep.

Irving followed the sleeping, vulnerable, Bob and stayed close while his abdomen was swabbed with Iodine.

He watched as a six-inch opening was cut into the right side above Bob's hip.

Blood was soaked up and intestines were moved aside, before being clamped out of the way to expose Bob's appendix.

"The last time I saw this much blood and shit the Luftwaffe had just bombed the latrines in Bari." The surgeon was considering the incised chasm in Bob's abdomen where his appendix had burst, leaking blood and flecks of faecal matter onto the surrounding organs.

"Might I get some suction in here?"

The surgeon removed his hands to allow a theatre nurse to apply a suction hose to the boggy contents around Bob's guts.

"Right, now let me yank this little bugger out of here so we can get on with sluicing this young man's innards clean."

Irving watched the surgeon go to work, fast hands deftly plucking, pulling and cutting into the pit within Bob's abdomen.

The appendix came out, a large purple, angry slug, and was dropped into a steel kidney dish.

A curved needle was drawn out of its packaging and handed to the surgeon in the teeth of long forceps, which was brandished like a wand.

He began tying the walls of the intestine where the appendix had once been.

Standing back to visually inspect his work, he tested the stitches with a probe before counting the instruments he had used.

"Where the bloody hell is my watch?" The surgeon looked at the assembled theatre staff, "My joke, now let's get these guts hosed down so we can all nip off early for a Brandy."

The whole operation lasted just under three hours.

Bob was wheeled out of theatre and into a recovery room where a variety of other patients were, by degrees, waking from the various procedures which had required induced sleep.

And there he was, My goodness me Grace was in the recovery room appearing through the walls of the hospital over to Bob's right.

Irving was up, ready for a show down, he could feel the energy balling up inside like the rage and disgust he had felt upon witnessing the Leecher draw out Bob's life force.

"Still alive then I see?" My goodness me Grace maintained the distance between himself and Irving, not moving from the patch of wall he had emerged through.

"What do you want?" Irving demanded.

He was too weak for a full-on fight with My goodness me Grace, he hoped his bluff and bravado would be enough to fool the Leecher.

He needed more time to prepare and recharge.

"I told you I'd be watching you Irving. I'm still watching you Irving. Don't let him out of your sight Irving, not for one second," His voice was like syrup, dripping with sickly sweet venom, "that's all it would take Irving, one second, then both of you would be gone."

My goodness me Grace hadn't moved from the spot, but Irving could swear he had grown larger with every word, he needed to pull out a wildcard.

"Don't threaten me," Irving growled, "I know what you are, I KNOW WHAT YOU ARE! AND I'M COMING FOR YOU!"

A nurse meandered quietly between the beds, checking pulses and respiratory rates before removing a bowl of balled up tissues and vomited bile from a man, who had woken with a swimming head that ballooned into nausea before rushing to empty his stomach.

The gamble appeared to pay off, My goodness me Grace withdrew into the wall slightly.

Irving advanced a little putting himself between Bob's bed and the wall which contained the danger.

"Be careful Irving, you're not strong enough for this fight." The retort caught Irving of guard, he faltered slightly, he gathered himself.

"Then what are you waiting for?" He hissed across the room at the wall bound Watcher.

A few moments passed in which Irving thought My goodness me Grace might launch his attack, long seconds waiting for his opponent to draw.

The attack never came, My goodness me Grace retreated slowly through the wall, much to Irving's surprise and relief.

Irving stood sentinel over the bed in which Bob was gradually regaining consciousness, My goodness me Grace had gone.

Irving had watched and waited for the ambush which never came.

He was satisfied that his bluster had been enough to give the Leecher second thoughts, for the time being.

This wouldn't last for long though and Irving knew that, if he was going to win this fight, he would need to get strong, fast.

Temptation

Bob's recovery was slow, he had been advised not to return to work for at least six weeks, and then only on very light duties.

No heavy lifting or straining for fear of ripping the stitches which held his insides inside.

He had obediently stayed in bed for the first few days, once he had been allowed to go home.

The bed rest had made his legs itch, he had graduated to laying on the sofa in the living room.

His mum had put the TV on for him while she got on with the work of keeping the farm house.

Irving had helped with the chickens on a few occasions but was reluctant for Bob to be out of sight for very long.

Bob lay on the sofa and read.

He imagined that, by the end of his six-week enforced rest, he might read enough to fill a small library.

The TV however held no interest for him and was just background noise for his mother's benefit rather than his.

Linda, the district nurse, had visited early on, to check his stitches and change the dressing.

Bob's mother took this as an opportunity to invite her for Sunday dinner, making it quite clear that she would not accept 'No' for an answer and insisting that Linda addressed her, informally, as 'Vesta'.

Sunday arrived with the rain, as a drum beat, to welcome the morning.

Bob took up his spot on the sofa while the house slowly filled with the smell of cooking, meat and vegetables mixed with the sweet cotton of a Victoria sponge.

The air was muggy making the clouds blister with heavy rain.

Bob's dad stepped through the door, cursing the mud which coated most of his right leg, right arm and up to his right ear.

He relayed the story, much to Bob's amusement, how he had been itching his foot on the tractor step.

His wellington boot had come loose and fallen off the tractor into the mud.

He had tried to make a grab for the boot and missed, throwing himself into the muddy field, while the tractor had trundled off.

Bob's dad had given chase, losing the other wellington boot in the process.

Bob's laughter had caught his mum's attention, she stood sternly looking at Bob's Dad, trying not to smile.

"Ken, if you make him split his stitches I shall bat you with the washing pole." The washing pole was a stout, tapered cylinder of wood, used to pummel dirt from fabric before they were removed from the caustic stew.

"Now get yourself out of that muck and dress for company, Linda is coming for dinner."

Linda had arrived draped in the heavy yellow, waterproof poncho before Bob's dad had finished washing the mud off himself.

Bob's mum had greeted Linda at the door and ushered her inside.

Bob could hear the commotion in the hallway of his mum fussing like a bantam.

"Doesn't she look lovely Bob?" Bob's mum had reappeared towing Linda, by the hand, through into the living room, "she made that herself."

Linda wore a green A line dress covered in white flowers and a white rounded collar.

"You look very nice." Bob commented slightly embarrassed at being put on the spot.

"Thank you Robert, you look very fetching in your pyjama's." She smiled at Bob who suddenly felt very under dressed.

"TA-DAH!" The awkwardness was broken by the reappearance of Bob's dad who was dressed for dinner in the suit, which had not grown with him, that he had been married in.

His hair was slick with pomade and had been combed in a severe side-parting, it looked like it had been set in a force-ten gale.

Bob's mum frowned.

"If you…" she started, then gave up, "come on Linda, you can help me in the kitchen."

Both disappeared through the door and were replaced by the sound of chatter and laughing.

"Careful boy, she'll have you married off before the day's done."

Bob's dad strode across to the television set and switched it on, "Shift up." He swatted at Bob's legs with a newspaper.

Irving felt a tingle.

He had been watching the scene in the living room from the relative safety of the sideboard which displayed crockery and horse brasses.

Bob hitched his knees up to clear a space on the sofa, which his father filled before giving Bob's knees a final swat.

The sounds of laughter from the kitchen were getting louder as potatoes were tested with the point of a small knife.

Bob's dad huffed in mock disgust before turning the TV volume up.

"Will you two be quiet, Farming Diary is about to start." He called over his shoulder towards the kitchen.

The laughing stopped for a second.

"What was that?" Bob's mum replied, before the laughing continued.

A distant rumble of thunder brought Irving his first revelation, he saw Bob struck by lightning which arced across the room from the television set to the sofa.

A flash followed, soon after by the crack of thunder as lightning tore at the air meant the storm was coming in fast.

Irving knew from the speed that the shiver took hold, that he didn't have long, he needed to get Bob away from the sofa quickly.

He moved towards Bob and, balling up energy in a static charge, delivered a measured jolt to the muscles which surrounded Bob's bladder.

The muscles obligingly contracted and induced an urgent need to pee.

Bob jumped to his feet,

"Got to go." He announced,

"And when you've got to go..." His dad began.

Bob went, scurrying along to the bathroom, fumbling with the bow which secured his pyjama trousers around his waist.

He made it to the bathroom when the lightning struck. There was a flash almost immediately followed by the roar of thunder, startling the two women in the kitchen and making Bob jump mid-pee.

"That sounded close!" Bob's mum looked at Linda who had yelped when the thunder struck,

"That was very close." Linda agreed, from the living room Bob's dad called out.

"It jumped out of the Tele." Linda followed Vesta into the living room.

"What's that Ken?" She asked

"I think it got me from the Tele." Ken replied, a little shakily.

"What got you?"

"The lightning, it jumped out from the Tele, and got me." Bob's dad was sitting bolt upright on the sofa, one hand gripping the arm the other in a tight fist at his side.

His hair, which had been held flat by the pomade, was stuck out like a strange dandelion, steaming slightly from the abrupt heat.

"Are you okay Ken?" Bob's mum sounded worried, "Should we call an ambulance?" She looked over at Linda.

"I'm fine Vesta, I think I'm fine, it jumped out of the Tele."

The television screen was grey, a scorch mark lined the glass with fine, root like veins.

Bob appeared at the living room door,

"What's happening?" He looked at the assembly in the room.

"Robert, you'll know, is lightning wet?" Bob's dad asked, still sitting.

"I don't know, I wouldn't have thought so, why?" Bob replied, still confused.

"Well, if it isn't then I've probably peed my pants."

"Then it serves you right for wearing your wedding suit, doesn't it?" Bob's mum retorted, relieved that her husband was still alive and seemingly in good spirits.

Linda set about checking Ken to make sure he didn't need hospital treatment.

His pulse was steady, his blood pressure was strong and, all in all, had got off lightly.

The remainder of the evening passed uneventfully, and Irving rested in the corner.

The conversation around the dinner table centred on Bobs' dads' close encounter with lightning.

Linda helped Vesta wash up the cutlery and crockery, while Ken and Bob set about moving the television set out of the house and into the yard.

Before leaving, Linda made Ken promise that he would visit the doctor's surgery for a check-up, just to be sure he hadn't suffered any residual effects from the lightning strike.

The next few weeks saw Bob recuperate fast.

The television set was replaced, as was the aerial which had melted into a warped sculpture that was still mounted on the roof.

The insurance company had refused to pay out due to the lightning strike being an act of God, Bob's dad had remarked that he'd have to have a word with the Vicar.

He eventually bit the bullet and picked a set with a slightly larger screen, so he wouldn't have to sit so close.

After five weeks' recuperation since the operation, Bob was ready to go back to work.

He felt as if he had read all there was to read and sitting at home on the sofa was beginning to make him irritable and restless.

Irving was also glad that Bob was getting out of the house.

Although the constant rest had meant that he could begin drawing again, albeit in small amounts, Bob was now stronger than he had been for a long time.

Irving was also stronger, he hadn't had to expend any energy for a long time as Bob's incapacity had kept him, pretty much, out of trouble.

The day Bob went back to work felt like a breath of fresh air.

At the print works, Wally had insisted Bob show him the scar, which was still complete with black, spindly stitches like spider's legs trying to escape from the crimson grin beside Bob's belly.

Ray had taken on the lion's share of the work, sending Bob on errands to the ink shed, or with samples for proofing.

At the end of the day, despite Bob's eagerness to clean down the inky spools, Ray would only allow him to hold the linen rags.

"I've been given orders Bob," Ray remarked, "I'm not to let you do any heavy lifting."

"Who's told you that?" Bob enquired, wondering if his mum had phoned the office prior to his return.

"That lady, the nurse," Ray answered, "she's fierce."

And that was that, Bob was back to work, but Linda had ensured that his convalescence would continue one way or another.

The wind had turned cold and Bob was regretting his decision to take a different route home.

It took him across the fields and passed a walnut tree, which he wanted to inspect for its crop and their ripeness.

The cold air pulled at his cheeks as it blew across him in gusts.

Bob had given up pedalling and was now wheeling the bike along the dirt pathway, which bisected the field like a faint smudge.

The tree stood, like a familiar friend, at the distant edge of the field.

The walnuts were still wrapped in swollen green buds.

The relatively cool summer, and abundance of rain, had convinced the tree to push out large bulbs in large numbers.

Bob could tell by the absence of tell-tale squirrel activity, that the nuts had not ripened enough for either him or the squirrels.

He reached up to grab a low hanging branch and was immediately reminded, by the pull at his side, that the stitches were not happy for him to attempt any acrobatics, regardless of what Bob thought. Propping his bike up against the trunk, he scanned the nearby floor for any stick, long and stout enough to suit his purposes.

It didn't take long to find a windfall which ticked all the boxes.

Brandishing the gnarly stick like a knight with a long sword, he set about unseating the walnut buds from the low branch with sturdy swipes, hitting the clutches of seeds with rhythmic determination.

Finally, a group of five, still attached to the twig, dropped a few yards from Bob's feet.

He dropped the stick and went to retrieve his prize, removing his pen knife from a trouser pocket with which to excise the nut from the pith.

A slice around the soft green meat exposed the hard shell inside.

He folded the blade back into the handle.

The folded knife was then used a hard wedge onto which the nut was pushed and twisted until the shell gave way around its circumference.

The seed inside looked good, it was big and healthy, no sign of disease or discolouration.

Bob smiled, the rest of the bunch was peeled and left whole before Bob planted them, some distance from the parent tree.

Arriving back at the farm, Bob noticed Linda's bike propped on its stand against the shed.

"Hello Bobby," his mum paused her conversation with Linda, who was sitting on a stool with Lucy on her lap, "would you like a cup of tea?"

She pulled a mug from the cupboard before Bob had answered.

"Yes please Mum," Robert replied before facing Linda, "you've made friends I see."

Linda smiled,

"Well, I knew you wouldn't say anything, so I had a quick word with your supervisor."

She looked sheepish in an unapologetic way.

"I meant Lucy." Bob motioned to the chicken on Linda's lap.

"Oh, right, yeah, I love chickens, this one's a real sweetheart."

Lucy appeared to be falling asleep.

"Ray said you were fierce." Bob smiled.

"Well, Ray knows what's good for him."

Linda lifted the chicken off her lap, stood up and placed the bantam down onto the warm stool.

"Let's have a look then, pop your shirt up." She gestured to Bob's stitches. "My word, one day at work and you've already popped one of your stiches."

Carefully reaching towards Bob's side, Linda plucked at the torn thread pulling it through the red, puckered pin prick.

"You have done well." She announced, holding the broken suture in the air as evidence.

"That must have happened at the walnut tree," Bob confessed, "when I tried to get a walnut." Linda looked unimpressed.

"If that wound opens, your guts will fall out. Walnuts or no walnuts you can't take me to the pictures with your guts hanging out all over the place can you Robert?"

Bob's mum giggled from the other end of the kitchen, as she removed a Victoria sponge from the oven.

"Bobby, drink your tea," his mum passed the mug to him, "now who'd like a piece of sponge cake?"

Lucy was back in the yard, cake crumbs had been collected into little handfuls and scattered for her and her feathered cohorts, to peck at in a flurry of activity.

Bob's wound had been redressed with fresh gauze by the time Bob's dad stepped through the door.

"Just the person," Linda got to her feet and retrieved her medical bag from under the stool, "kill two birds with one stone."

"Oh no you don't," Bob's dad made a show of running away, fumbling to put his boots back on.

"It's witchcraft I tell you."

Wellington boots flopped around as Ken ran in a circle, before slumping down on the sofa.

"Do what you will."

He conceded defeat and allowed Linda to shine a small torch into his eyes, check his pulse and measure his blood pressure.

"I'll be back next week to take those stitches out Robert, unless you pop them all before then," Linda turned to Bob's dad, "I don't think there's any hope for you Ken, you're beyond medicine." Everybody smiled as Bob's mum accompanied Linda to the door.

The chatter continued until the district nurse pedalled toward the road, and Bob's mum finally closed the door.

The next couple of weeks flew by.

Linda removed Bob's stitches under the proviso that he would stay on light duties for a further three weeks.

During those three weeks, he would also take her to the cinema to see Send me no flowers, staring Rock Hudson and Doris Day.

Bob agreed, figuring that light duties referred to anything which was within his capabilities and the film, about a hypochondriac who thinks he is dying, might turn out to be quite entertaining.

The cinema date had been set for Saturday.

On Friday afternoon, after work, Bob set out across the field armed with a hessian bag.

He had several lengths of bamboo cane tied to the crossbar of his bike, a piece of copper pipe fashioned into a hook and more than enough garden twine.

He headed for the walnut tree.

The scar on his abdomen was still pink and fresh but had stopped complaining against all but the most strenuous exertion.

However, the cold, damp air had managed to settle on his chest and would bring about fits of coughing if it caught him right.

The fruits on the tree had begun to swell and split, bearing the walnuts to the world and tantalising the squirrels which had started to eat in earnest before the winter.

At the foot of the tree Bob assembled his apparatus, bound together with oddments of string and wire.

The bamboo canes were grafted together as one, then topped with a copper hook.

The tree prepared its self for the onslaught.

The joined canes were raised aloft, and the hook positioned above a branch which held bunches of ripe nuts.

Once in place Bob covered his head with one arm and shook the branch vigorously for fifteen seconds.

The hard rain fell, thudding around Bob's feet and cracking him on the arm, hands and head before ceasing when Bob stopped to collect his haul.

The nuts were quickly peeled and checked, before being deposited in the rough bag.

For the next hour, Bob continued this ritual.

Moving to a new spot under the tree before encouraging a new cascade to fall on his head.

Irving looked on wondering if the self-inflicted bruises, Bob was collecting, would be anything to worry about in the future.

Eventually the tree-hook was disbanded and strapped to the frame of Bob's bike once again, it was getting dark.

The bag of nuts was folded over on its self, and the top tied with a length of twine.

It hadn't been a bad haul.

The bag felt heavy, once zipped into his jacket.

He engaged the Dynamo against the rear wheel of his bike, knowing that the evening would close in before he made it back to the farm.

The next morning Bob woke with a woolly feeling in his head, the cough had taken hold and brought a wheezing rattle to every third, shortened, breath Bob took.

Irving had been careful, he hadn't drawn too much from Bob since the operation, the faceoff with My goodness me Grace had left him feeling vulnerable and weak.

The onset of Bob's chesty cough had scuppered Irving's plans to start a nightly draw which would see him back to full strength, or as near as damn it.

He was glad that My goodness me Grace hadn't called his bluff.

It would have been over fast, Bob was weak.

Irving was weaker, he knew the Leecher would have taken them both apart without too much effort.

But Bob was in no condition to provide the life force, which Irving would need, to protect them both and he was stuck without any answers.

Waiting and hoping the Leecher had forgotten about him was not an option, he needed energy and he needed it fast.

Irving could only see one avenue left open to him.

Other than drawing from Bob, which would leave him too weak to fight the chest infection and probably not provide Irving with enough energy to fight off an assault.

He would have to draw from someone else.

Irving had wrestled with the idea from the moment it had arrived.

To draw from a stranger was to become the thing he despised the most.

The thing which he was fighting against.

He would become a Leecher, the thought sickened him.

He hated himself for allowing the consideration to form.

But there was no other way, to fight this thing he would need to become this thing.

Irving hoped there would be a way back.

It would be risky, the council already had their suspicions about him.

To prove them right would, without doubt, be terminal for Irving, he was still under curfew and had to stick to Bob like glue.

The opportunities to draw from another human were few and far between and, although Irving knew there was no other way, he hadn't managed to stomach the thought of becoming the beast.

He experimented on mice to begin with, drawing their life force into his own, moving onto rabbits and pigeons.

The surge was too fast to control, leaving lifeless corpses to fall off their perches or roosts, casting them into the brief abyss of decay.

It was too much to control, once he had started drawing, Irving couldn't limit the surge of raw energy that pulsed through him.

It wasn't enough, the tiny drips of energy were nothing compared to how much he would need to stand a chance against the Leecher.

He had briefly wondered about drawing from a cow, the larger beast would have greater energy reserves than the creatures he had sapped already.

The cow idea seemed to have merit, it did however present Irving with two problems.

Leaving Bob on his own was out of the question, both for Bob's sake as well as his own and coercing Bob into a cow field would be no mean feat.

Secondly, if Irving couldn't control the energy surge, there would be the matter of cows dying in fields for no reason.

Dead cows would undoubtedly draw attention from both humans and Watchers alike, in fact anything domestic or bigger than a rabbit was going to draw attention to Irving.

Something he could do without.

He wondered whether he could draw from a human and stop before he drew too much.

Maybe that was why the Watchers were bound, the energy was familiar.

The bound human was important so the draw was measured, it had to be.

The Leechers drained their prey, not because they hated humanity but more likely because they didn't care.

They didn't have to control the draw because, to them, the human didn't matter.

Revelation

Bob's cough had grown worse throughout the day.

A gnawing ache had settled in his lower back and sent a twanging sting up his spine every time he coughed.

He had peeled the walnuts and arranged them on a tray next to the fire hearth to dry.

The nights were beginning to chill, the wet weather called for damp clothes to be draped over a cage, and left to dry overnight, in front of the fire.

Bob had been given a shot of brandy to shift the cough and an M&B tablet to ease his sore throat.

He had sat in the chair next to the fire, it had settled into dull orange hue that peeked through the ashen kindling and scorched fossils of coal.

The sound of the door knocker brought Bob out of a light semi-sleep, he looked first at his dad, then in the direction of the front door.

"I'll get this one." His father announced, smiling. "Friend or foe?" He called out in a booming voice, raising his chin to help the message carry.

Bob strained to hear any reply.

There was a silent pause, then the muffled voice of Father Molyneux started, stopped, then after the creak of the letter box opening began again, a little clearer.

"Um, friend I think, it's Father Molyneux. I just popped over to see how you're all doing."

"Come right on in Vicar," Ken boomed, "the doors not locked, and we've already hidden the silverware."

The door opened then closed, followed by the ruffle of Father Molyneux's removing his coat closely followed by Father Molyneux himself.

"Ahh, good evening Kenneth, Robert, how are you both? I'd heard you've both been under the weather recently, so to speak." All three men smiled.

"Very good Vicar, very sharp. As you can see I'm in shockingly good health." The vicar smiled appreciatively,

"Touché Kenneth, a very nice riposte, let's hope this conversation doesn't become too charged."

"Will you two clowns stop playing silly buggers and someone peel these bloody potatoes, excuse the language Father." Bob's mum was standing in the kitchen doorway brandishing a vegetable knife.

"My apologies Vesta, I was just enjoying some puns with your good husband here." Father Molyneux looked slightly crest fallen.

"Well you should know better Father." She passed the knife to Bob as he made his way to the small bowl of muddy potatoes, "How are you feeling Bobby?"

"A little bit better," Bob coughed, "throat's not as sore." Bob replied, leaving his father and the vicar to restart the conversation without him.

"Something's brewing," More towels announced, the two Watchers had positioned themselves away from the thoroughfares that crisscrossed the living room, "the Council is worried, they still haven't gotten any closer to getting this Leecher and the community is getting restless."

Irving considered for a moment,

"I think I know who the Leecher is," there was silence, "it's someone on the council." Irving ventured, both Watchers shifted uncomfortably.

"Well?" More towels prompted, finally breaking the pause which Irving had created.

He was still unsure whether imparting his knowledge, onto another member of the Council, was a good idea at this precise moment.

"I think My goodness me Grace is the Leecher." Irving conceded with an air of relief.

"Are you sure?" More towels asked, "He's on the National Council, how could he possibly be a Leecher?"

"Maybe he's not." Irving had thought through the possibilities and come up with a solid theory.

"Not what?" More towels asked, confused by the unexpected direction Irving had taken.

"Not a member of the Council. I mean My goodness me Grace is or was a member of the Council, but what if My goodness me Grace isn't My goodness me Grace?"

"You're not making sense Irving," More towels was more confused, "what are you talking about?"

"Does anyone on the District Council know My goodness me Grace? Have you met him before?" It all made sense to Irving, the more he explained, the more convinced he was that he was right.

"The Council sent for him, the National Council said that he was on his way." More towels confirmed.

"You know that, I know that, maybe the Leecher knew that too, maybe the Leecher got to My goodness me Grace before he got to us."

"What you're saying is My goodness me Grace isn't My goodness me Grace, he's the Leecher." There was a hint of understanding from More towels now, Irving's revelation beginning to fit together.

"That's what I said," Irving continued, "he's shifted the suspicion onto me to cover himself, he's threatened me, and we had a standoff in the hospital after Bob's operation." Irving knew More towels was beginning to understand.

"Have you told anyone about this?" More towels asked, mulling it over again and weighing up the possible next moves.

"Just you so far," Irving confirmed, "I wasn't sure whether I could trust anyone on the Council."

"What happened at the hospital?" More towels asked and listened intently while Irving ran through the events in more detail.

The facts were interspersed with Irving's hypotheses, both Watchers nibbled at the bits of jigsaw which didn't fit until the case against My goodness me Grace was as strong as they could make it.

"We need proof." More towels conceded, "We need to catch him in the act but we're going to need a plan." More towels was concentrating, trying to pull it all together.

Finally he returned his focus on Irving, "Leave it with me, I think I have an idea." He announced, "Stay close to Bob; don't leave his side until I get back to you."

Irving felt better although the tingle had been faint, it had been there for a while now, almost fading into the background.

Now Irving had an ally and between them they were coming up with a plan.

Two weeks later Bob found himself in the hospital again.

The cough had taken hold to the point where Doctor O'Connell was worried that it had progressed to full blown pneumonia, he had quickly referred Bob to the Hospital.

His mother had prepared an overnight bag containing fresh underwear, socks, three spare shirts, a spare pair of trousers, toothbrush, toothpaste and a tin of Cornish mint humbugs.

The hacking cough came in fits, striking little fires of pain around Bob's chest and lower back, easing off, leaving him exhausted and light headed before returning for fresh torment.

Each bout of the hacking, wheezing, rasping cough sent shudders through his body.

They were so violent that Bob was worried that the needle end of the drip, which now jutted into the crook of his right arm, would be ripped out, spraying blood over the walls, floor and ceiling of the men's ward and his co-inhabitants.

The bed on Bob's left contained Mr Nelson, an elderly gentleman who had suffered a stroke and subsequently lost the use of most of the right side of his body.

Bob had tried to engage him in conversation on the afternoon of his arrival but, what little Mr Nelson had to say, Bob found difficult to understand through the slurred mumble.

To Bob's right, next to the stand which held the drip aloft, was Mr Fattore, an Italian prisoner of war who had found the life in post war Britain so amenable that he decided to stay.

Mr Fattore had married a school teacher before setting-up an art shop in a small village a few miles to the north of Cambridge.

During the lengthy conversations whilst waiting for food, medication or the sporadic blood samples, Bob had discovered that Mr Fattore had recently suffered from a spate of dizzy spells.

One of which had caused him to fall over mid-moustache waxing.

The fall had sent him head long onto the edge of the sink and left him concussed and very badly bruised.

Over mint humbugs and cups of tea, the bedfellows discussed their lives, football, politics and interesting anecdotes, swapping obscure facts which they had collected over the years.

Mr Fattore sketched one of the most striking fountains, which Rome had to offer, on a sheet of headed hospital notepaper.

Horses erupting from the basin whilst Neptune locked in combat with a furiously defiant octopus.

As the week wore on Bob's cough got steadily worse, he was finding it impossible to pull in a lungful of air and to complicate matters further he was running a fever.

Initially the high temperature was brought under control with paracetamol but as Saturday approached, Bob's condition continued to worsen.

On Friday evening, it was decided to infuse the I.V. drip with penicillin to try and bring the chest infection under control.

Irving was worried, he was still weak and with Bob's condition deteriorating he didn't dare draw anything from him, if he was faced with a fight he would need to fight with his wits.

Although My goodness me Grace didn't know how weak Irving was, it wouldn't take too long to figure out that he was almost running on empty.

Irving knew that a sustained attack would almost certainly finish him off.

He would need to think outside the box, avoid head on confrontation, he hoped More towels would come up with a good plan fast.

Saturday came and went, Bob's condition got worse a lot faster than was expected.

He would wake, shivering in pools of sweat, shaking and hacking until it looked like he might burst.

The Doctors increased the dose of paracetamol as well as the dose of penicillin, trying to claw back some of the lost ground.

It appeared that the infection, rather than rolling over, was fighting against the antibiotics and more importantly, it was winning.

On Sunday Bob had a visitor, Father Molyneux sat in the chair next to Bob's bed while Bob slept in beads of sweat.

Irving was pleased to see More towels, especially as More towels had good news, he had a plan.

"You're going to have to be ready at a moment's notice Irving," More towels had explained the ambush, how he had laid false information with the council to bait My goodness me Grace out of hiding, "he's going to strike fast so you're going to have to be faster, once we've got him in the act there can be no hesitation, if you don't get him first he'll drain Bob then he'll drain you."

More towels' words were chilling, they reminded Irving how fragile he was, how fragile Bob was and how unready he was for, what might turn out to be, this final faceoff.

He wanted to tell More towels how weak he was, how unready he was, how if he just had a little more time he would be stronger, more able to fight.

There was no more time, Irving knew the time was now.

Father Molyneux had been sitting at Bob's side for a little under two hours when the doctor came through on his rounds.

He checked the chart at the foot of Bob's bed, checked the drip and the times noted when penicillin was added.

He checked Bob's pulse and looked at the declining chart that mapped Bob's blood pressure.

He tapped the pen against the top of his front teeth before making a note on the chart to increase the penicillin once again.

Father Molyneux waited until the doctor looked as if he was satisfied that he was finished before approaching.

"Excuse me Doctor, I wonder if you could tell me how Robert, this young man," he gestured in the direction of Bob's bed, "is getting on?"

The doctor examined Father Molyneux for a few seconds, "Are you family?" He asked abruptly.

"He's a parishioner, it would mean a lot to his family if I could bring them some news." He looked hopefully at the doctor who had been checking his watch.

"Well, right now he's dying, we're not sure why but we're doing as much as we can to keep him alive. We could use some help Vicar, maybe you could have a word with your boss, a bit of divine intervention wouldn't go amiss right now." Father Molyneux looked crushed.

"Oh, oh okay, thank you doctor, I'll tell his mother and father that you're doing all you can." The doctor softened a little,

"Say a prayer for him vicar, he can do with all the help he can get right now." He smiled then continued his rounds.

Father Molyneux sat back down next to Bob, tapping his knee nervously he looked over at Bob.

"Hear that Robert? You'll be right as rain in no time." He bowed his head and began to say a prayer quietly.

Irving had waited by Bob while people buzzed around the ward, checking temperatures, administering various pills and potions or just visiting family and friends.

The evening faded into night and the shift of nurses and doctors changed, one team gladly making way for the other.

Irving had watched, waited and thought about his predicament, about the plan, about the Leecher and about You bastard Henry, he looked on as Bob slept.

For the first time since Bob's resurrection, everything seemed hopeless.

He was too weak, Bob was too weak.

The plan was hurried and relied upon My goodness me Grace being distracted by Bob, long enough for Irving and More towels to get the jump on him.

But it was the best plan they had, and Irving was desperate.

Bob's mouth was dry, the room was dark and unfamiliar.

he could hear noises, snoring, nearby.

His pyjamas clung to him damply, he felt cold and needed to pee.

He moved the bed covers and immediately felt a stabbing pain clawing in his right arm, he was attached to something which, now unbalanced, fell to the floor with a crash, pulling at Bob's arm once again.

A light came on next to him, a man in a bed next to him looked over at him,

"Are you alright Robert?" The man asked, sitting up in bed.

"What is this? I need to go; I have to be home." Bob's mind was darting around trying to find answers to the avalanche of questions, which demanded answers the second he had woken up.

In the dim light, Bob could see a shadow standing over him at the foot of the bed.

The shadow was tall, nearly touching the ceiling.

The darkness was uneven, like looking at a shadow through the ripples on a pond, it moved towards him.

"What are you? Are you …?" Bob asked his voice dry and cracked, "Why have you come for me? I'm not ready. Who are you?" He asked again.

From the next bed, the man spoke.

"I'm Angelo Fattore. Are you okay Robert? Should I call the nurse?" Bob was paying him no attention.

He was fully focused on the apparition that was slowly moving towards him, through the foot of the bed.

"Nurse!" The man next to him had begun shouting, "Nurse, Infermiera! Infermiera! Mio Dio siete tutti sordi? Infermiera!"

The shadow was at Bob's feet, he drew his legs up toward his chin when a jolt of static electricity snapped at his toes, the shadow was hissing.

Very slightly and right on the edge of hearing, like the static on the TV the hiss modulated and changed in pitch ever so slightly but enough for Bob to recognise his name.

The warmth on his arm made Bob look down.

The bed sheets and floor near his bed were scarlet, his blood was oozing from the rend in his arm where the needle had been yanked out.

The room spun away into a dark tunnel, like Bob was falling backwards into a fuzzy well, he felt dizzy and sick then nothing.

The nurse who had responded to the shouts from the ward switched the lights on, sitting up very animated, in his bed was the Italian.

"Mr Fattore..." The nurse began, about to chastise the unruly patient.

Then she saw Bob, the drip stand laying across the floor in a puddle of diluted blood and the bright red stain which was spreading over the white bed linen.

She moved, going over to the dry side of Bob's bed she pressed a red button above the light fixing above Bob's head.

Then, after retrieving cotton wool and a roll of gauze, she set about staunching the blood which was still dribbling out of the arm.

That done she then began counting a pulse.

The sound of hurried 'clip, clip, clip, clip' footsteps was followed by a second nurse, who surveyed the scene from the door way with an unmistakable air of authority.

She looked back down the hallway toward the owner of a lighter set of 'clip, clip' footsteps and issued a set of orders.

"Call the duty Doctor, then bring a mop in here."

Irving watched the flurry of activity, which was growing like a roman candle around Bob, he was going to have to be on top form tonight.

He knew that it wouldn't be long before the needles and tourniquets would start flying like startled sparrows, he would need to be watching for any that might inadvertently end Bob's life.

"He saw me again." Irving thought.

"He's burning up." The senior nurse had wiped the sweat from Bob's forehead with a cloth and now felt his brow with the back of her hand.

The first nurse recorded Bob's pulse on a chart, reporting to the second nurse that his pulse was "a little slow."

A third nurse came in with a mop and bucket on wheels which squeaked every time one of the wobbly wheels, briefly touched the floor.

A few minutes later the Doctor arrived, changing the balance and softening the urgent tension a little. The third nurse was wringing out the mop head with a miniature mangle, that had been fastened to the bucket.

The drip stand had been stood back up and Bob's arm had been wadded and wrapped, to stay the bleeding.

The Doctor took up position at the side of the bed and started checking Bob's pupil dilation as the senior nurse brought him up to speed with the events so far.

She removed the thermometer from Bob's armpit and checked the mercury.

"One hundred and three." She announced, the Doctor looked up and raised an eyebrow.

"Let's get another line in, then get some paracetamol in him to control that temperature and get some Benzodiazepine in there to calm him down."

He looked over his shoulder to the nurse who was retreating with the mop and bucket.

"Call ICU, tell them send up a couple of porters with a trolley and get a bed ready. Robert! Can you hear me Robert?" The Doctor pinched the skin on Bob's neck and got no response.

When Bob came to he was in a different ward.

He had a room to himself, he lifted himself up a little and shifted back in the bed slightly to have a look around the room.

It was more like a cubicle with walls but no door, his clothes had been placed in the cabinet next to the bed and his arm stung, like he had been given an intense Chinese burn.

He felt numb, a little sick and extremely tired.

Closing his eyes, he laid back in the bed, hoping that the sickness would fade.

His head felt disjointed, like someone had jumbled up all his memories.

Then for good measure, strapped heavy diving weights to his arms, legs and body.

Everything was an effort.

He was aware that someone was in the room with him, but couldn't summon the effort to open his eyes and tilt his head.

There was a cold sensation in his left arm followed by needles, a million needles stabbing at his arm, little jabs.

Bob heard a groan, it sounded like him but from a long way away.

"Are you awake Robert?" The nurse had spoken to him, it must have been his groan, "I'm just giving you some Penicillin to try and kick your infection, you might feel a little groggy because of the sedatives."

The stabbing ran up his arm into his shoulder and down his arm into his fingers, hot spikes of pain that made him feel hot and cold at the same time, he must have groaned again.

"You gave everyone a bit of a scare last night, do you remember?" Bob didn't remember.

He was too busy trying to work out how to stop the incessant pain, which was moving steadily into his chest.

Bob was dead.

Irving could see it, there was no obvious cause, he was just lying in the bed motionless, all life force gone from him.

The shiver had started just after he'd become aware of the tingle, that was a bad sign.

The tingle was usually his thinking time, the space he needed to think clearly before the shiver came on and signalled his 'doing' time.

This time it was too fast, he had no thinking time, he was in the doing phase without knowing what to do, once again he felt helpless.

He had searched the vision of Bob's demise, for a clue, something to focus his direction but there was nothing, no useful information for him to mould into actions.

In the corner of the room Irving felt lonely, he looked on as the nurse pumped more antibiotics into the drip above Bob's right shoulder.

Bob looked grey, as if the proximity of death drew not only the life but also the colour from a person.

Irving remembered being paired with Bob, the words of the Promises which he had spoken but not really understood.

He remembered his drive to divine, to collect enough energy to propagate the future with one of his own, how he had used that energy to give Bob life when it had been stolen by the Leecher.

That was the essence of the promise, Irving understood now.

He had chosen a direction, he would use his life to keep Bob alive for as long as he could.

He was too weak to fight.

The only real chance Bob had, was for Irving to keep him alive for as long as possible.

Irving waited for the nurse to leave before he moved to the side of the bed, he gently touched the points on Bob's neck, from where he had drawn energy so many times before.

He pushed against the urge to draw once again and forced the energy back into Bob, not much at first but then coaxing more through.

Irving stopped and withdrew to the corner of the room, he could hear familiar voices.

The Vicar and Bob's parents were making their way down the corridor, the doctor was with them.

He was trying to explain what had happened last night that had led to Bob's move into the Intensive Care Unit.

Bob's Mum had been crying, her shoulder gripped supportively in Ken's hand, his arm across her back.

Nodding occasionally in response to the Doctor's explanation, Father Molyneux walked a few paces behind, he looked tired, clutching a small Bible to his side.

Irving watched as they entered the cubicle and lined up against the bed, looking down on Robert, pale and still, his breathing shallow and slow.

Vesta swept Bob's hair to the side of his face as she looked down, hoping for signs of recovery or recognition.

Father Molyneux began leafing through the pages of the small Bible, hoping for divine inspiration or intervention.

The Doctor stood just inside the entrance to the cubicle as a nurse brought in another large syringe in a kidney dish and made notes on a chart before taking Bob's pulse, recording his temperature and blood pressure.

"What's she doing?" Bob's Mum looked from the nurse, who had begun emptying the syringe into the clear bag which hung above Bob's bed, to the Doctor in the doorway.

"We're giving Robert high doses of antibiotics to help fight the infection, we're hoping that, once we bring the infection under control, Robert can start to recover."

The nurse withdrew the needle before withdrawing from the room.

Bob could feel a fresh surge of pain, tearing through his arm starting in his elbow.

It ripped and grabbed at his body, piling new pain on top of old pain, blasting into his flesh and bones in merciless waves.

The cold followed, adding to the discomfort.

Then nausea, the bile in his stomach burning up into his throat, the acrid acidic stench filling his nose in a private torment.

Bob moaned again, his Mum bent over closer to his ear,

"Hi Bobby, your Dad's here as well, the vicar too. You're going to get better you hear? The Doctors are doing all they can to make you better okay?" Irving noticed the colour draining from Bob's face, leaving him a yellowy grey, his face looked hollow.

Bob's Dad must have noticed it as well.

"Why's he gone that funny colour Doctor?" He asked, slightly confused.

The Doctor ventured further into the room, drawing alongside Bob just as Bob began to shake.

The tremors were light at first, like the shiver that runs down your back when you get out of bed onto a cold floor on a crisp Autumn morning.

They grew in magnitude to become an uncontrollable quake of trembles and spasms.

"Peter Molyneux? Is that you? As I live and breathe, it is you."

Everyone turned to look at the broad figure who filled the entrance of the cubicle, the Vicars' look of puzzlement was quickly replace by one of recognition.

He apologised to Bob's Mum and Dad before handshaking the man out of the cubicle, and down the corridor, where they would be just out of earshot of the muted tones he now adopted.

"My goodness me Calum, it's lovely to see you again, I wish it were under better circumstances, what are you doing here?" Father Molyneux was still shaking the other man's hand, a slow, firm and sincere greeting.

"I work here," Calum replied, "I'm a consultant to the head of Cardiology, I see you managed to stay on through Curacy."

"Indeed, I did," the Vicar replied, "but it appears you did not."

Calum laughed and slapped priest on the shoulder.

"Too fond of sins of the flesh Peter." He conceded in low hushed tones, "What brings you here? One of your parish?" He indicated to the cubicle.

"And a friend," said the Vicar, "it's not looking too good I'm afraid."

He looked sullen, almost crest fallen.

"Nonsense Peter, if the good lord has deemed it right that I should bump into you in this place, at this point in time then there must be a reason," Calum lifted the priest's shoulders, almost hoisting him off the ground, "let's take a look at him."

And off he strode, past the Vicar and in to the cubicle.

Father Molyneux followed.

In the cubicle, the Doctor already looked put out as the consultant flicked through the charts and notes.

He had begun to demand that Calum explain himself before Calum shut him down.

"Are you responsible for this?" Calum waved the clipboard in the air in a gesture towards the bed.

"I'm this man's Doctor. Who the hell are you?"

"Can't you see you're killing him?"

The question was blunt, Bob's Mum and Dad looked on from their son's bedside with a look of shocked confusion.

"What do you mean?" The doctor still hadn't steadied himself fully but the accusation that he was killing his patient had put him on the back foot.

"Nurse!" Calum bellowed over his shoulder, "bring me a fresh bag of saline and get that shit out of his arm."

"That's my patient!" The doctor had regained his standing and was on the front foot once again. Calum looked up, straightened, walked over to the doctor and sharply slapped him across the cheek, leaving the instant white mark to quickly fill with a red blush.

"This man is allergic to Penicillin. You might as well have been feeding him rat poison you damn fool."

He brought his face close to the doctors.

"I'll be submitting a report with my full recommendations but from this point on this man is my patient, now get out of my sight." The doctor looked flustered but left the room without another word.

Calum turned to Bob's Mum and Dad who still looked shocked.

"I'm sorry about that," he said, addressing them with a nod, "Peter can vouch for my credentials, now let's see about giving Robert a fighting chance."

The next twenty minutes saw the room full of activity, nurses changing drips, bringing cups of tea for Bob's Mum, Dad and the Vicar.

The Vicar had initially declined but was grateful of the warm sweet drink when it arrived regardless.

Irving looked down at the bed from the corner of the room, as the flurry and bluster was orchestrated and conducted by the consultant.

He snapped out his wishes in a manner, which made Irving feel, that they had already been carried out but the world hadn't caught up yet.

The colour had gradually returned to Bobs face and his breathing had become deeper and steady.

Calum indicated to Vesta and Ken who obliged by stepping into the area of the room he had indicated, before he shook them by the hand in turn.

"I'm sorry for my unorthodox entrance," Calum paused briefly and took a breath, "but desperate times call for desperate measures, and I believe that had I not have acted in the manner which I did your son would be dead. If not now, then certainly by the end of today."

Bob's Mum looked shocked, Calum continued.

"Robert is allergic to the antibiotic, Penicillin, which was being pumped into his body. It was supposed to help Roberts body to fight the infection, but Roberts allergy meant that his body was having to fight on two fronts. At the rate it was being pumped in, it was a fight Robert was never going to win."

"Why did he look so yellow?" Ken asked.

"Jaundice," Calum replied, "Robert was going into shock, his internal organs were shutting down and his liver had all but given up."

"Will he be okay?" Vesta asked, her voice shaky and broken.

"He's not out of the woods by a long stroke but we've given him a fighting chance." Calum took Vesta's hands in his own, "If he improves enough overnight, I've ordered an abdominal x-ray for midday tomorrow. Once we've had a look at that I think we'll be in a better place to make some progress."

He flashed an encouraging smile at Bob's parents,

"If you would both like to go home and get some rest, I'm sure that, when you pop back tomorrow Robert will be feeling more like himself. By the look of his medical records he must really like it in here." Calum's face softened into a warm smile.

"He is very accident prone," Bob's mother explained in defence of her son, "do you really think he'll be better tomorrow?"

"Robert's a fighter, he's been through things which would have killed lesser men, I'm sure he'll be in good spirits tomorrow.

If you like, I will take your telephone number, so I can keep you informed of any changes in Robert's condition."

"Well if you're sure, if it wouldn't be any trouble." Vesta started shuffling through her hand bag in search of a pencil and piece of paper.

The consultant retrieved a pocket book from his jacket and a pen from his breast pocket which he offered to Ken.

Irving watched as the room gradually emptied, the nurses gradually left, eventually followed by Calum, Peter, Vesta and Ken.

Leaving Irving and Bob to themselves, Bob asleep and Irving weakened but glad that the shivers and visions had subsided.

Bob was alive.

The Truth

Bob woke up feeling groggy, his body ached but the sharp shards of pain had gone, he sat up carefully and looked around.

Next to him, on a small cabinet, was a small glass and a pitcher of water.

Bob was thirsty; his teeth felt furry, he wondered how long it had been since he had last brushed them.

Careful not to dislodge or jolt the rubber tube, which connected him to the clear bag on the stand next to his bed, he poured half a glass of water and began sipping it slowly.

Enjoying the coolness which slid down his throat.

Bob could hear a trolley being wheeled somewhere along the corridor.

The smell of cold toast, powdered eggs and tea told him it was breakfast time.

His stomach grumbled.

He still felt ill.

The cough in his chest, although slightly less violent, was still strong.

Every breath he took was punctuated with a whistling wheeze, followed by the rattle of mucus from deep within his lungs.

The jagged darts of pain which flew around in his abdomen had not eased any either and he was still feverish.

The beads of sweat on Bob's forehead and sudden shivering chills made it plain that he was still, very much, 'In the woods' and probably wouldn't be out of them for the next few weeks.

But the smell of the food, combined with the gnawing emptiness that was Bob's stomach, had lifted his spirits and whetted his appetite.

Gradually the trolley got closer until finally, looking to Bob's eyes like the Arc of the Covenant, it stopped at the entrance to his cubicle.

"Breakfast Sir?" Two men pushed the trolley, the younger of the two looked a little older than Bob. The other, older man was much older, early sixties maybe, close to retirement, it was the younger man who had asked the question.

He lifted the lid from the hot plate to reveal crisp rashers of bacon, there were powdered scrambled eggs and cold toast.

A large urn stood on the lower level of the trolley with the word "TEA" proudly emblazoned on its side.

Bob wondered how long it had been since he had eaten last.

Whether the bacon would take on an extra succulence because of the length of his abstinence and whether the golden toast would melt in his...

"Nil by mouth." The older man announced, looking above Bob's bed.

"Whaaa...?" The younger man's question was cut short by the older man's answer.

"Nil by mouth, on the sign you plum, look on the sign." He pointed over Bob's head, the younger man looked up at the wall.

On a small blackboard, screwed to the wall was written 'Nil By mouth' followed by 'Allergic to Penicillin' in large red chalk letters.

"Oh yeah," the younger man looked a little stunned, "Sorry." He offered Bob by way of an apology.

Then the trolley was gone leaving Bob with the sound of rattling and the feeling of emptiness.

It wasn't long before a second trolley had collected up the tea cups and breakfast crockery.

A nurse arrived in Bob's cubicle.

"Good morning Robert, how are you feeling?" She began by putting away a large thermometer and retrieving a smaller one. "Would you pop this under your tongue for me." She instructed, offering the thermometer to Bob's lips like a mother bird with a very frozen worm.

Bob obliged.

"Why amuh I Niw by mouff?" He asked, trying his best not to rattle the glass rod against his teeth too much.

"You've been booked in for an X-ray at eleven o'clock, the consultant made it very clear that you were not to have anything to eat before the X-ray."

She secured the cuff round Bob's bicep and began squeezing the little rubber bellows, inflating the cuff and listening to Bob's arm through a stethoscope.

"Not even a piece of toast?" He asked forlornly.

"Not even a little piece." The nurse confirmed, deflating the cuff and releasing Bob's arm.

"Oh," Bob felt as deflated as the cuff which now lolled about as it was folded up and stowed, "well what time is it now?" He asked.

"It's nine twenty-three." She showed him the upside-down fob watch as proof.

"That means I have to go hungry for almost two hours." Bob was sure that he might have starved by then.

"Tell you what, why don't I bring you a fresh jug of water?" She asked buoyantly trying to improve Bob's mood.

"Can you put a slice of toast in it?" Bob replied, disheartened by the mornings developments so far.

"You are funny." The nurse smiled, got up and left the cubicle.

A few minutes later one of the orderlies returned with a jug of water and a fresh glass.

The morning dragged on for Bob, it was punctuated by various sample takers wanting blood or urine.

One even stuck a swab down his throat for good measure, but the brief periods of activity were broken up by longer periods of inactivity.

Bob began to wonder whether he would ever taste toast again.

"Maybe toast doesn't exist," he mulled over the theory in his head, "maybe toast is just a hypnotic suggestion and I only think I like toast, but toast has never been a real thing."

Bob thought about it, he didn't remember being hypnotised but that could just be down to the skill of the hypnotist.

"Toast, toast, toast." The more he said it, the sillier it sounded.

Irving wondered if it was the fever or whether the recent events has just been too much as he watched Bob, lying in bed staring at the ceiling, repeating the word 'Toast' at different speeds, in different accents and finally accentuating different syllables.

Irving was glad when the monologue was broken by the arrival of Bob's Mum and Dad, accompanied by the consultant.

"Calum McAllister, pleased to meet you Robert." The man rushed over and shook Bob by the hand.

"Morning Bobby, how are you feeling?" Bob's Mum looked worried but relieved that her son appeared to be much better.

"Alright lad?" His Father nodded.

"Umm, I'd like some toast." The consultant looked confused for a moment.

"Of course you would, wouldn't we all?" He beamed a smile over to Bob's Mum. "All in good time Robert, first we have to get you better." Bob looked on slightly confused.

"We need to get you X-rayed so we have a better idea of what's going on in there," his smile was confidently reassuring, "once that's done I can work out a plan of attack and soon enough you'll be right as rain. Then it's toast all round, what do you say Robert?"

"Umm, okay." Bob replied.

The consultant spoke so fast that Bob didn't know if he had heard the words or just felt them as they whizzed past.

He looked over to his Mum, she was smiling at him, so it must be okay.

"Okay." He said again but with a little more confidence than the first time.

More towels arrived to see Irving a few minutes before the porters arrived to take Bob to the X-Ray department.

"You have to go and meet the council," More towels blurted out before Irving could greet him.

"Right now, it's urgent." He added.

"What's it about?" Irving asked, "Is this part of the plan?" unnerved by the sudden arrival of his friend and the urgent summons from the council.

"No, I don't know what it's about, I was just sent to tell you that the council wants to see you now." More towels seemed flustered.

'This cannot be good' Irving thought to himself. He started to move, "What about Bob?" Irving asked, not wanting to leave Bob's side for a moment.

"I'll watch over Bob," More towels replied with certainty, "he'll be fine."

"What about Father Molyneux?" Irving asked.

"He's in the Hospital chapel, honestly, it's fine now just get going!"

Irving left, passing through the hospital walls, heading directly for the Library as fast as he could, without using too much energy.

It was a long hike.

Irving had been careful, not to use any energy unnecessarily, up until now.

The council met in the Library in the town a few miles outside the city limits.

'What could it be about?' He wondered, silently slipping between the pedestrians.

With all the recent events this was something he could do without.

'What if My goodness me Grace was at the meeting?' The prospect of confronting the Leecher released a caterpillar of fear within Irving, which wriggled around inside him.

He couldn't fight him, Irving knew he was too weak, hopefully the other council members would protect him.

"We can end it if we all stick together." Irving said to himself, still not convinced, he hoped Bob would be okay.

"Right Robert, I'm afraid you're going to have to wait in the corridor until the Radiographer gets back from her fag break." The porter said, wheeling the gurney parallel to the wall and applying the wheel break. "Shouldn't be long now."

More towels caught up with the group who had stopped outside the heavy double doors to the X-Ray room.

He checked back along the corridor they had just come from, there was no sign they were being followed, that was good.

"So far, so good." He thought to himself.

"Move away."

The instruction came from My goodness me Grace, More towels spun round to face him.

My goodness me Grace stood a good ten meters away at the other end of the corridor.

More towels wondered if he had been watching him the whole time, the way he had just popped out had taken him by surprise.

"It doesn't have to be like this," More towels advised, hoping to avoid a confrontation right now, "just turn around and go, we can both forget you were here."

His words had an edge to them, offering a warning and a way out for them both.

"I can't do that," My goodness me Grace replied steadfast, "you know I can't do that."

"Then what are we waiting for?" More towels announced, then sped along the corridor to rush the Watcher who waited at the far end.

The Tannoy speaker on the wall, half way along the corridor, crackled with static.

The two porters looked up at the sudden burst of feedback.

"Speaker system's on the blink again." One commented,

"How much they spend on them things?" The other added,

"Too bloody much." The first replied, leaning back against the wall.

A tall, thin lady appeared from the far end of the corridor.

Yelping with surprise as a static charge jumped with an audible 'Snap' from the brass light switch into her elbow.

She approached rubbing the elbow,

"I heard that from here," the first porter remarked, "must be a storm on the way."

"Must be the wiring on the way out." The woman retorted, "who have we got here?"

Irving had made it to the edge of the city, there was an incline ahead of him.

It was the only real hill in the area.

When it snowed in the winter, children from across the neighbouring towns and villages would pick a spot at the top.

Brandishing commandeered tea trays and purpose built sledges, with the simple focus of getting to the bottom as quickly and as noisily as humanly possible.

Now it just offered its self as another obstacle for Irving.

Both combatants knew this would be a fight to the end, they stalked each other neither wanting to make a wrong move.

More towels lashed out, a whip of energy snapping across My goodness me Grace.

He hopped back, not managing to avoid the lash, before bursting forward with a counter that left More towels stunned.

He shook it off, knowing that he could not give his opponent the edge, clawing through the other with a draining attack of his own.

"Irving! Irving! Stop Irving!" Irving stopped to face the sound of his name, it was Are you alright Mortimer.

"I was just coming to see you," Irving started, "you wanted to see me."

He was confused by Are you alright Mortimer's sudden and unexpected appearance.

"Yes, yes, I'll explain on the way, now we must get back to the hospital, I'm afraid we may have put you and Bob in some danger."

They turned and headed back in the direction Irving had just come from, Irving moving as fast as he dare.

"What do you mean 'put us in danger'?" Irving asked, slightly lost within the jumble of events.

"Well, we know who the Leecher is," Are you alright Mortimer announced, "but we needed some bait to draw him into the open." He continued.

"I, well, we know who the Leecher is too." Irving conceded excitedly, "What do you mean by 'Bait'?"

"We, well, we used you and Bob as bait," Are you alright Mortimer confessed, "it was the only sure-fire way to flush him out. That's why we need to get back to the hospital."

"It's okay," Irving felt a little relieved, "More towels is with Bob, he'll stop him."

"Stop who?" Are you alright Mortimer sounded alarmed.

"My goodness me Grace." Irving explained.

"What?" There was real confusion in Are you okay Mortimer's reply.

"The Leecher, My goodness me Grace is the Leecher."

"Don't be so ridiculous, My goodness me Grace isn't the Leecher, I've known him since I was divined. He may come across as a little odd but he's the only one I could trust to look out for you." As the realisation began to sink in, Irving started to feel sick.

"More towels is the Leecher." The pieces had started to fit into place.

"Took a lot of digging, managed to find a Watcher who knew of Father Molyneux, turns out he never had a Watcher." Are you alright Mortimer explained.

"So, More towels isn't More towels?" Irving was still trying to understand how he had been completely taken in.

"More towels is More towels, but Father Molyneux never had a Watcher. Never even had a brother for that matter, let alone a twin."

They were close to the hospital now.

"It turns out that More towels drained his bound human as well as the twin brother when they were both babies. Turned on the other Watchers too, they reckon he drained half a dozen before they chased him out of the area."

Irving was shocked, he could still picture the vile pulsing parasite standing over Bob.

"Seems More towels figured he'd be better hidden in plain sight, so he latched on to Father Molyneux to give himself some credibility."

The hospital was in front of them.

"Worked too, we even put him on the local council." Are you alright Mortimer sounded embarrassed.

"I left him alone with Bob." Irving announced, feeling a real fear of what he might find. From behind the two Watchers, a church clock struck Eleven.

"Robert, have you had an X-ray before?" The tall radiographer looked down at the paperwork that had been passed on the her by one of the porters.

"Yes, quite recently as it happens, I broke my ribs a few months ago." Bob replied.

He had been watching the dust motes, which seemed to be drawn to a sweet spot along the corridor a few feet away, like iron filings to a strong magnet.

"Oh yes, here we are," said the radiographer, reaching the relevant notes in Bob's medical history, "what were you doing under a combine harvester?"

"Praying." Remarked Bob.

"So, another chest X-ray," She had looked through the notes and deciphered the X-Ray requisition, "we're going to need to get you a shield." She added, motioning to the porter to wheel Bob into the X-ray room.

Bob was positioned under the machine.

The film was placed in a drawer under the trolley and a heavy lead apron was placed over Bob from the waist down.

The Radiographer then clicked a switch that turned on a large, illuminated cross hair.

Bob felt as if he was about to be bombed as the target of an RAF sortie.

My goodness me Grace knew that More towels was getting the better of him, he was stronger,

much stronger.

He gathered himself, setting up for a counter attack, after a series of heavy blows had landed and really taken their toll.

More towels was firing off lots of strong attacks, he had more energy to waste than My goodness me Grace.

For every three attacks which My goodness me Grace avoided, the one that got through would more than make up for.

He ducked away from a whip of energy that More towels had lashed across the room and arced one of his own back in reply.

This to-ing and fro-ing of energy would end up draining him completely, leaving him at the mercy of More towels.

My goodness me Grace hoped that Are you alright Mortimer had found Irving and was on his way back.

The next strike sent My goodness me Grace sprawling across the floor, it was over.

The crosshair was adjusted, slightly up, slightly left then focused on Bob's chest and upper abdomen.

The radiographer retreated into a small booth behind a thick wall.

"Right Robert, I'm going to ask you to lay very still and hold your breath until I tell you to breathe freely, okay?" Bob signalled that he understood and was ready to go.

"Right, now deep breath in and hold."

More towels loomed above My goodness me Grace, the raw energy bubbled and pulsed like a bruise.

"It's not about the leeching, or the easy energy," More towels was towering above My goodness me Grace, the final blow ready to be delivered.

"It's about this moment, this power every time I stand over one of you about to fade, I love this feeling, I don't think it will ever get old."

He was sneering down at the beaten Watcher who, by now, was powerless to defend himself.

Irving and Are you alright Mortimer flew through the walls, appearing in the corridor in time to see the younger porter kicking the tiles underneath a red 'No Entry, X-ray in progress' sign which glowed from within.

"He's in X-ray." Irving flashed down the corridor, passing through the walls towards the X-ray room, closely followed by Are you alright Mortimer.

The room exploded with energy, sparks of energy fizzed around the walls, bounced off the floor and crashed down from the ceiling.

The cacophony was like a million symbols being scraped along a million chalkboards at a million miles an hour.

There was no escape, My goodness me Grace willed himself to fade, the pain was too much to bear but the end did not come.

More towels, swollen with energy and rage, was flung onto the floor of the room against the wall of the booth.

The room hissed and spat like an angry cat, claws at the ready.

Irving was first through the wall into the room, Bob was alive, laying on the trolley.

His relief was cut short at the sight of My goodness me Grace lying prone on the floor, close to fading.

It was quickly replaced with anger as he saw the palpitating purple mass of the Leecher on the floor at the other side of the room.

Are you alright Mortimer burst through the wall behind Irving a surveyed the scene, it was mesmerizing.

Both Watchers were stunned by the chaos, the noise of dissipating radiation and of their fellow Watcher fading on the floor in front of them.

The revolting parasite, who had brought about all this misery, staggered at the bottom of the far wall.

 The two watchers stood and starred, transfixed by the whole scene, they didn't react to the Leecher as he pulled himself upright, the effects of the X-ray blast beginning to wear off.

"Get him Irving." Bob whispered from the trolley, it was only a whisper, but it brought Irving out of his trance.

He charged at the Leecher, the rage spilling over, carrying him forward like a typhoon.

He caught More towels full on, crashing them both onto the floor, pinning him to the tiles.

"Irving, I was..." More towels began,

"No!" Irving growled back, plunging into the Leecher, "I don't want to hear it."

Irving tore the energy from the Leecher, the draw was torrential, flooding Irving with more power, more anger.

Driving him further, faster, pushing him to extinguish this monstrosity which had destroyed his friends.

Then he felt it, just a twinge at first, but growing stronger by the second, unmistakable in amongst the rush of energy.

There were memories.

You bastard's memories, Bob's memories, My goodness me Grace's memories and an infinity of other whom he didn't recognise.

Irving reasoned, they were probably the memories from the other victims of More towels' ravenous appetite.

Irving stopped drawing from the Leecher, he looked down at More towels who was close to fading.

"I'm going to destroy you," Irving told him, "but before you fade I want you to know something. I want you to see something, and remember as you fade to nothing, you gave me this More towels."

He got up and moved to where My goodness me Grace lay on the floor.

Are you alright Mortimer had knelt by him, offering his presence as comfort to the fading Watcher,

"What are you doing?" he demanded as Irving stooped over My goodness me Grace and reached into his centre.

"Watch." At first Are you alright Mortimer thought Irving was leeching, finishing off his friend.

He readied himself to defend the stricken Watcher, but quickly realised that this was different.

The flow of energy was going the wrong way, it was passing from Irving into My goodness me Grace, little by little the Watcher got stronger.

"How are you doing that?" Are you alright Mortimer was awe struck by what he was seeing.

Drawing from a human was an everyday occurrence, draining from a Watcher was common for a Leecher.

He'd never heard of, let alone seen, a Watcher turn everything on its head and push life into another Watcher.

"You taught me this," Irving wanted to be sure More towels was watching, "YOU taught me this, the day you killed Bob!"

Are you alright Mortimer was stunned,

"He killed Bob?" He looked flustered, "But how's he?" My goodness me Grace got up from the floor, much to Are you alright Mortimer's surprise.

"I'm sorry My goodness me Grace, I thought you were the Leecher."

Irving was moving towards Bob, More towels laughed weakly from the floor.

"Thank you, Irving." My goodness me Grace replied, checking himself over.

Irving reached into Bob and began pushing energy back, the same way he had when Bob had lain lifeless on the ground.

"You gave me a gift More towels, I can give life. I'd like to thank you by making sure you can't take any more, from anyone else."

195

Irving stood over the fading Leecher ready to deal the final blow.

The Leecher looked up, full of loathing and contempt.

"I'm not alone, Irving," the Leecher was still laughing, "there are more of me than you can imagine." He hissed, "You make me sick, all of you make me sick." He was fading fast, "You're all so weak."

Then he was gone.

Irving drained him completely leaving the white floor tiles, where More towels used to be, ever so slightly yellow.

"What just happened?" Are you alright Mortimer was completely lost.

"How can he see you?"

"How can Bob see you?"

"Can he hear you?"

"What did you mean when you said he killed Bob?" Are you alright Mortimer was not alright, he had lots of questions about what he had just seen and heard.

Irving gathered himself, Bob was being wheeled out of the X-Ray theatre.

"I'll try to explain but I'm not leaving Bob."

Irving followed the porter with the wheelchair out of the room and along the corridor, the other two Watchers were close behind.

"How can he see you?" My goodness me Grace asked, "he said your name! Looked right at you and said your name."

"I'm not sure," Irving admitted, "I think it might have started when I divined into him after More towels had killed him."

The revelation brought about a new range of questions from both Watchers, Irving patiently answered as best he could.

Going through the finer points as Bob was wheeled back to the ward, then eventually back to the X-Ray room to have the whole procedure repeated, due to a blur which had appeared on the first image.

Are you alright Mortimer explained that, when he had suspected Irving would be targeted by the Leecher, he had tasked My goodness me Grace to guard Irving and Bob, just in case the Leecher struck.

On the mend

Bob had lost two-thirds of his liver, the X-ray had shown a space under his diaphragm which should have contained his liver and now was full of, how had Doctor McAllister put it? 'Liver pate'.

The first X-ray had failed, Bob was sure he hadn't moved or breathed while it was being taken.

The Radiography department had blamed movement for the blurring on the film so the whole procedure had to be repeated.

Including the wait for the film to be developed, then analysed, then handed over to Bob's doctor. The decision was made to drain the fluid from Bob's abdomen.

A hole was made in Bob's side and a clear pipe positioned to syphon off the infected gloop that had been holding back Bob's recovery.

Dangling down, from the side of Bob's bed was a bag, looking like an oversized hot water bottle, which contained some of the, two-thirds of Bob's, liver which had been liquidised.

"I've got to be in here for two weeks!" Bob looked beseechingly at his mum and dad in turn,   "Two more weeks!"

"Well, if that's how long you need to get better, that's how long it will take." Bob's mum was relieved that her son was feeling better and seemed restless to get back to the farm.

"What's the food like?" His dad asked, eager to know whether his son was eating better than he had been.

"It's not all that bad." Bob replied, thinking back to the sausages, scrambled egg and buttered toast which he had eaten that morning, and which was still evident by the small yellow dab on the white bed sheet.

Two weeks was going to drag, Bob was already feeling claustrophobic.

Having to lay very still was not as relaxing as it ought to be, especially when any movement made the tube wiggle inside him.

At least his mum had brought him some more books to read.

He had resorted to battling the crossword puzzle in an old newspaper left by one of the orderlies which, a little to his surprise, he had found quite compelling.

Doctor McAllister had been a regular visitor to Bob, during his rounds and Father Molyneux had brought grapes, on the two occasions that he had been ministering to the sick and bereaved.

The speed of Bob's recovery was amazing,

"You were all but dead," Doctor McAllister had admitted during one of his visits, "once they stopped poisoning you it was almost as if your whole body switched back on again."

Bob was glad to hear it, he had felt much better once they had started to drain his liver.

Now he was eager for them to remove the tube and let him get back to the farm.

Two weeks wouldn't be over soon enough.

Irving stood before the full council once again, nervously looking at the row of familiar faces who stared back at him.

Are you alright Mortimer started the meeting.

"Thank you for coming Irving, I trust you will be able to stay until the end this time?" It was light hearted, but Irving could tell that Are you alright Mortimer wasn't joking.

"Um, yes, I'll try my best." Irving conceded.

"The rest of the council has seen the report made by myself and My goodness me Grace, this is your opportunity to add anything you feel we might have missed, okay?" Irving nodded that he agreed and understood.

The report was clear, concise and bore little resemblance to the events which happened in the X-ray room.

There was no mention of More towels draining My goodness me Grace, no mention of Irving reviving both My goodness me Grace and Bob.

There was also no mention of Irving dealing the final draw, which faded More towels to nothing more than a stain on the tiles.

Irving sat patiently, answering questions in the vaguest possible manner, as he had been instructed by Are you alright Mortimer.

On a few occasions the question had to be fielded by My goodness me Grace, when Irving's answer strayed a little too close to the truth for comfort.

The three Watchers had agreed that the exact details, of what they had witnessed Irving do in the X-ray room, needed to stay in the X-ray room for everyone's good.

A sanitised version of events had been set out and agreed upon by all three Watchers.

Now Irving was trying his best not to let, even the tiniest hint of, the cat out of the bag.

Bob was bored, his parents had gone home, leaving him to his diminished sprig of grapes, half read book and completed crossword puzzle.

He had been looking around the room and shifting his legs, which had grown too hot under the bed sheets.

Wiggling his legs up and down had drawn the cool air into a brief pocket between the sheets and mattress and offered Bob some respite from the warm stickiness under his knees.

The undulating sheets had thrown his crossword pencil onto the floor a few feet from the bed, Bob had watched it for half a minute then devised a plan, that involved a rolled-up newspaper and a well-aimed swat.

The first few attempts were fruitless.

The pencil was just out of reach of the flailing broadsheet baton.

Bob leant out of the bed a little further, the next attempt caught the end of the stranded pencil, making it jump but bringing it no closer.

He leaned out a little further.

There was a tingle, Irving stood up.

"I'm really sorry," he said sheepishly, "I really, really have to go." And disappeared through the library wall.

Bob is now in his seventies, he is married to Linda and still enjoys playing bowls.

To date he has survived:

Two hernias

Rheumatic fever

Being run over by a combine harvester

Being pronounced dead after a car accident

A burst appendix

Gall stones

Penicillin poisoning

A heart valve replacement

A triple bypass

Pneumonia

The loss of around two thirds of his liver

Kidney infections

Skin cancer

Falling into a large patch of brambles

And numerous other injuries which, without Irving, would have made this book more like a health and safety pamphlet.

About the author:

Andy Scoville very rarely refers to himself in the third person.

He lives in a large village in East Anglia, along with his partner, Paula, two children, Lily and Charley and Paula's parent's Bob and Lin (who live in a 'shed' in the back garden).

He has two dogs and loves peanut M&M's.

He can be contacted at: andy@thenaughtystep.net

29464716R10122

Printed in Poland
by Amazon Fulfillment
Poland Sp. z o.o., Wrocław